MURDERED
BY
PLASTIC SURGERY

A High Desert Cozy Mystery - Book 5

BY

DIANNE HARMAN

Published by: Dianne Harman
www.dianneharman.com

Interior, cover design and website by
Vivek Rajan

This is a work of fiction. Names, characters, places, and incidents either are the product of the author's imagination or are used fictitiously, and any resemblance to actual persons, living or dead, business establishments, events, or locales, is entirely coincidental.

ISBN: 978-1548350918

CONTENTS

ACKNOWLEDGMENTS

To the four women who were sitting at the bar in Armando's restaurant in Palm Desert: Thanks for being the inspiration for this book and prompting me to let my imagination run wild!

To my readers: I so value you, and I thank you for your continued support, your feedback, and your ideas for future books.

To Vivek: Thanks for always making sure that my book covers are so visually appealing, my books are well-formatted, and all the other technical things that you do so seamlessly, and which, quite frankly, are beyond my technical abilities!

And lastly, but certainly not least, To Tom: Thanks for always being there with encouraging words, ideas, and thoughts that help make each of my books as good as it can be!

Win **FREE** Paperbacks every week!

Go to www.dianneharman.com/freepaperback.html and get your FREE copies of Dianne's books and favorite recipes immediately by signing up for her newsletter.

Once you've signed up for her newsletter you're eligible to win three paperbacks. One lucky winner is picked every week. Hurry before the offer ends!

PROLOGUE

The neatly framed sign hanging on the wall in the reception room of Dr. Keith Ramsey was a quote attributed to Diane Gerber, a well-respected plastic surgeon in Chicago.

"No one can or should tell you why you should consider plastic surgery for aesthetic reasons. You should be able to clearly define your desire to improve aging or to enhance facial or body appearance. Others may support you in your decision, but the decision to have plastic surgery should be yours alone."

Dr. Keith Ramsey was one of the leading plastic surgeons in the Palm Springs area, and that was saying a lot in a city that was known as a mecca for people who wanted that type of surgery. Although the sign hanging on the wall in his reception room said the decision to have surgery was solely that of the patient, he didn't completely subscribe to that line of thought. Instead, he often urged his patients to agree to the surgical operations he recommended, after promising the patients it would greatly enhance their beauty.

The enormous sums of money he reaped from performing such optional surgeries helped pay for the alimony and child support payments the court had levied against him in his second divorce.

He'd said good night to his administrative assistant, Sybil, the last person to leave the office suite in the upscale section of Palm Desert

1

with shops that rivaled those located on Rodeo Drive in Beverly Hills. The handsome middle-aged plastic surgeon sat at his desk in the early evening twilight and looked out the window at the desert hills as they turned from pinks to dark blues. He knew he was looking for excuses not to go home, so he delayed it a little while longer, checking the daily schedule for the upcoming week on his computer.

He never heard the door to his office being quietly opened or the swish of the scalpel as it was shoved with great force between his shoulder blades. The single deep stab wound was fatal, and he died almost instantly. His perfectly chiseled features were without expression, as he slumped over on his desk. The six women scheduled for surgeries the following day would have to find a new plastic surgeon. Dr. Ramsey's operating days had come to an end – an untimely end.

CHAPTER ONE

Marty Morgan-Combs called her sister and said, "Laura, I just finished the appraisal of the Shaker furniture collection Dr. Ramsey has in his home. I'll meet you at Armando's restaurant in twenty minutes."

"Perfect. I'll leave the office now and meet you there."

Twenty minutes later as Marty approached Armando's, she marveled at how the City of Palm Desert had succeeded in creating its own version of a Beverly Hills Rodeo Drive, with shops such as Escada and Baccarat, to name just a few. Given the sky-high cost to rent a shop in the area, Marty figured that as unpretentious as Armando's was, it must have been there long before the city fathers had wooed the prestigious shops which now lined the street. Trying to find a place to park on El Paseo Boulevard was a nightmare. "Woo Hoo!" she shouted involuntarily a few minutes later as she pulled into a parking place directly in front of the popular restaurant.

I'm taking this spot, and Laura will just have to use her psychic ability to find a spot as good as this one. May not be a very sisterly thought, but when it comes to finding a parking place on El Paseo as good as this one, it's every woman for herself.

To look at Marty's sister, Laura, no one would guess she'd been part of a study many years earlier at the University of California for

1

people believed to have psychic abilities. The study had confirmed that Laura definitely possessed extrasensory powers which allowed her to innately know things other people didn't.

Laura was attractive and dressed as any other insurance executive dressed – no fortune teller turban for her. She wasn't the least bit surprised that the study by medical experts had confirmed what her family had known since she was a small child, that she possessed some type of psychic ability which she often used to predict the outcome of future events. Marty had learned long ago that if Laura said she shouldn't drive down a certain street, she'd be well advised to take another route.

Laura lived in one of the four houses she owned that were located in the hills above Palm Springs. The houses surrounded a central courtyard where the residents gathered in the early evening to share the events of the day as well as communal meals. After Marty's divorce, she moved to California and rented one of the houses from Laura. She'd recently remarried and her husband of several months, Detective Jeff Combs, now lived with her along with her loveable, but sometimes neurotic black Labrador dog, Duke. One of the other houses was occupied by Laura's longtime significant other, Les, and the fourth house was occupied by John, who operated a business called the Red Pony Food Truck. John was a highly talented cook and he generally prepared all the evening meals for the residents of the compound, so he could use them as guinea pigs to try out new recipes he wanted to serve in his food truck.

*****

Marty opened the door of Armando's and quickly scanned the seating area for an open table. There was only one table available, and it was towards the back of the room. The bartender looked over at her and said, "If you want to eat, you better take it. That's the last one there is. We've got a full house today."

"Thanks," Marty said as she walked by the bar, noticing that every bar stool there was occupied as well.

So much for the doom and gloom economy the talking heads on television keep stressing, she thought. *Maybe the word hasn't gotten out to the people who like to eat good Mexican food at a fair price.*

She'd just sat down and picked up the menu when the front door opened, and Laura walked in. Marty stood up and waved to her. Laura joined her a moment later. "Are they giving away free food today or what? I've never seen Armando's this busy. I was really lucky to find a parking place, although it looks like you didn't have any trouble finding one."

"I have to admit the parking fairy was sitting on my shoulder when I found the one out in front. As to why it's so busy in here today, I have no idea," Marty said, "but I think we're lucky to get this table, even if it is in the bar area. I've only been here a couple of minutes, and I know I could have sold it several times over to people who wanted to eat here and were told there would be a wait."

"Well, considering how I've been fantasizing about one of Armando's chimichangas ever since you called me, I never would have forgiven you," Laura said laughing.

A few moments later chips and salsa were placed on their table. "Have you decided what you'd like to order?" the handsome young waiter asked in a lilting Spanish accent.

True to her word, Laura answered, "Yes. I want a chimichanga and a glass of iced tea."

"I'll have two beef tacos, and a glass of iced tea as well," Marty said, handing the waiter her menu.

"Your orders will be out in just a few minutes. I'll bring your drinks now."

"I wanted to tell him to ask the cook to hurry it up, since I'm starving," Laura said, "but I figured with this crowd it probably wouldn't make any difference. I imagine the kitchen staff is working at maximum capacity as it is. So, how is the doctor's appraisal coming along? I told Dick I was having lunch with you, and since he referred the doctor to you he's curious as to the status of the appraisal."

Over a year ago, Laura had insisted that Marty move to her compound in High Desert, California, when Marty told her she was getting divorced after finding out that her husband, Scott, had been having an affair with his secretary and wanted to marry her. Laura had told Marty she was certain Marty could make a go of her antique appraisal business in the Palm Springs area, particularly since Laura worked in the division of an insurance company which oversaw the insurance needs of wealthy people. Since wealthy people often wanted to let people know they were rich and tended to make their homes showcases to that effect, there was no lack of high-end items that needed to be appraised for insurance purposes in the greater Palm Springs area.

Laura's boss, Dick, was the one who decided whether or not a customer's household furnishings needed to be appraised before the company would issue an insurance policy to them. Often, antique collections were a part of an appraisal, as was the case with Dr. Ramsey's appraisal. Fortunately, Dick and Marty had hit it off, and he had given her as many appraisals as she could comfortably handle.

"The doctor has an incredible collection of Shaker furniture and other decorative items. I've seen a few Shaker pieces here and there, but I've never seen a home completely furnished with authentic Shaker furniture. I haven't had a chance to research the values yet, but anytime you have an authenticated piece by Isaac N. Youngs, you know it's worth a lot of money. I'm just curious what led the doctor to start collecting Shaker items. I could understand it a little better if he lived on the East Coast, but why here in the California desert?"

"I take it you haven't asked him."

"No, he's been all business the few times I've been with him, and I also get a sense things aren't terrific between the doctor and his wife. It's nothing I can put my finger on. I've only met her once, and it was very briefly. She came into the room the first morning I was there, and the doctor introduced me to her, but I had the feeling they weren't very happy together."

Marty stopped talking and took a bite of the taco the waiter had placed in front of her, at the same time looking at the large chimichanga on Laura's plate. "My dear sister, if you eat that whole thing, I would imagine the insurance company will not be getting any work out of you this afternoon, plus I think you're going to end up taking a long nap on the couch in your office as soon as you get back to work. Don't think Dick would approve of that, although if the chimichanga is half as good as this taco is, I'd understand."

"It is, and I hope Dick understands," Laura answered. "The gastronomic dreams I've been having this morning have just been fully realized. Now I have to convince John he needs to serve this at The Red Pony, so that way he'll try it out on us at the compound. Maybe I could say it needs this and that, and then he'd feel like he had to make it several times to get it right."

"Laura, that is really cold and conniving of you. John's cooking is the best, and if you said something like that to him, he'd probably end up in therapy."

"You're right. It was a momentary fantasy and certainly no reflection on his cooking. I was just trying to figure out a way I could have a chimichanga like this on a weekly basis."

"Well, considering Armando's has been around for a long time and probably will continue to be, you can always get one here." With that, they both became quiet while they enjoyed their meals.

A few moments later, Laura said, "So you're having thoughts about plastic surgery. Would I be right?"

Marty put down her taco and looked at her. "What makes you think that?"

"Well, I wish I could say it was my psychic abilities, but actually I had to sign for that expensive eye cream and neck moisturizer the FedEx delivery truck brought to the compound yesterday. I figured you were having some sort of mid-life crisis." She looked expectantly at Marty to see what her response would be.

Marty looked over at the bar and at the other diners sitting in the room, as she tried to avoid meeting her sister's eyes. Finally, she turned to Laura and said, "Yeah, you're right. I guess I'm scared. I mean Jeff is the most wonderful husband any woman could ever want, and that's the problem. Let's face it, I'm middle-aged, I look it, and Jeff is very attractive. I've seen how other women look at him, and I worry about what would happen if he decides he'd be better off with a younger woman, someone who didn't have wrinkles around their eyes and on their neck? All you have to do to find a beautiful young woman in this town is take five steps in any direction." She looked expectantly at Laura to see what her response would be. Laura noticed that Marty's eyes were shiny, and she seemed to be close to tears.

Laura took a sip of her iced tea and began to speak, "Marty, it's been my experience that one of the most attractive things a woman can have is self-confidence in her looks and an acceptance of just who she is. At this stage of the game, you might as well own those lines, because they've made you into the person who attracted Jeff in the first place. If you start being afraid because you're getting older, what message do you think you're sending to him? I'll tell you what that message is. It's almost as if you're telling him it's not acceptable if he gets a little middle-aged paunch or grey hair. It's like you're negating the man he is because you won't accept where you are in life. Does that make any sense?"

Marty thought for several long moments and then said, "I guess you're right. I'd never thought about it like that. I imagine it comes from doing this appraisal for a plastic surgeon. I mean, the man has two floor to ceiling bookcases full of pictures and books of beautiful women. It's been a little intimidating, to say the least."

"I'm sure it has, but fortunately you're beautiful in your own right. You don't need to go under the knife to try and regain what you looked like when you were twenty years old. All you need to do is look around you. I've heard there are more plastic surgeons in the

Palm Springs area than anywhere else in the United States, and based on some of the disastrous results I've seen, it looks to me like some of those doctors didn't really excel in medical school or in their residency."

CHAPTER TWO

As she continued with her conversation regarding plastic surgery and how she'd observed that some operations were less than successful, Laura said, "If you doubt what I'm saying, take a look at the woman sitting at the bar with those three other women. Her lips look like the ones I recently saw in some television documentary about rural tribes in Africa. Some of the women in those tribes use something called a lip plate to make their lips really big, particularly their lower lip. Evidently the bigger the size of the lip, the bigger the dowry a bride can expect to receive on her wedding day. In some tribes, the larger the lip, the greater number of cows the bride's father can demand for his daughter's dowry."

"Laura, although that sounds really weird, I'll bet some men like that look."

"Maybe, but I bet the father of that woman sitting at the bar could demand a whole herd of cattle and get it if this was Africa, and not Palm Springs."

"That's a little harsh, even for you, Laura, but I do have to say she looks like the poster child for a facelift that may not be quite what she intended. I remember one time Scott and I were at the airport in Cabo San Lucas, Mexico, on our way home after some R and R in the sun, and an older woman walked into the terminal. I felt sorry for her, because it was obvious she'd recently had a really bad facelift. As taut as the skin was on her face, I couldn't figure out how she could possibly close her eyes or her lips. Sleeping at night must have been a real challenge. Poor thing. I guess in some cases having a facelift not turn out to be quite what you'd envisioned would be really depressing."

The two of them resumed eating while the conversations from diners and those at the bar swirled around them.

"Laura, listen," Marty said, "the woman at the bar you were talking about just mentioned Dr. Ramsey. See if you can pick up what she's saying."

There were four women sitting at the bar, and it was obvious from the raised decibel levels of their voices they were easily on their second or third round of margaritas, although one of them appeared to be drinking a coke. They were all about the same age, in their mid-40's, dressed in yoga pants and lightweight designer tee shirts, and all of them wore designer running shoes. Marty estimated the combined value of the large diamonds they were wearing on their ears and fingers would easily match the cost of providing housing for several families. It was obvious these were women of means who didn't have to work to afford the baubles that adorned them.

"Okay, girls," the one Marty had referred to earlier said, "I'd like you to quit ignoring the elephant in the room. Today's the first day I've had the courage to show my face in public since Dr. Ramsey butchered me. I noticed everyone in yoga class stealing looks at me and from what I could see, they had pity in their eyes. So, Chelsea, Olivia, Tracie, what do you think?" She took a big sip of her margarita and sat back on her bar stool in a defiant manner.

The three other women exchanged quick glances, and then one of them began to speak. "Brandy, I'm sure you're being overly sensitive. You look fine, honest. I'm sure you're worried about your lips, but look at the movie stars. All of them have big lips. Anyway, you always have been your harshest critic."

Marty noticed that the woman who was speaking had deftly put one hand behind her back, crossed her fingers, and wiggled them so the woman sitting next to her could see what she was doing.

"I may be my own worst enemy, Olivia, but right now I'd give anything to look like I did before I went to that butcher. Mitch stopped by last night to bring me my monthly alimony check rather than mailing it. I'd be willing to bet he just wanted the satisfaction of seeing me look like this, considering it's the first time he's ever delivered it to me in person. It didn't make me feel very good, I can tell you that."

The woman she'd referred to as Olivia said, "Brandy, sure, your lips are big, but that's what's in style now. Lots of women are getting their lips done, just so they'll look like a movie star. Think of it as being fashionable."

"Olivia's right," one of the other women said. "It's no big deal. I'll bet most of the women in Palm Springs have had a little work done, and in some cases, a lot of work done."

"I don't mind that people can tell I've had some work done, but what bothers me is that I look like a freak. I just wish there was some way I could make that smug rich doctor feel like I do. I've thought about suing him, and I even made an appointment with an attorney, but he told me I didn't have a case, because I still look good. What he doesn't realize is that I don't look like the old me. It's as if the doctor was conducting some kind of an experiment and wanted to make me look like somebody else."

She continued, "From the way the doctor looks, I'm sure he's had some major work done on his own face. I hope the next time he goes under the scalpel, it slips, and he winds up looking like I feel. Actually, death might be too good of a thing to wish on him."

"Brandy, be careful. That's not something you want people to overhear. You don't look the least bit freakish, and like your lawyer told you, you still look great, and from what you're always telling us, men have never been a problem for you. As good as you look now, I doubt that it ever will be a problem. Speaking of which, how is that guy you've been seeing?"

"I don't know. I haven't had the courage to let him see me since the surgery. I'm supposed to meet him for a drink this evening at Tommy Bahamas, you know, the one down the street from here. We usually meet at a hotel and then, well I don't need to fill in the gaps, but given what I look like, that may no longer be an option."

"Brandy, the men you see don't really want a granddaughter. A daughter is enough for them, and you still look like every man's dream of a daughter."

"Thanks. I know Richard is pretty old, but I hope you're right," she said in a loud voice. "Actually, I think we've all had enough to eat and drink for today. We could probably use a little nap before the cocktail hour, wherever any of us plan on spending it. Chelsea, you're still our designated driver, thank heavens. Are you about ready to leave?"

"Yes," she said looking at her watch. "I've got an appointment with my attorney in an hour. Gabe's making noises about going to court to get my alimony reduced. Fat chance he'll have of doing that, considering I know the numbers of all of the secret bank accounts he keeps in the Cayman Islands. I haven't played that card yet, but I sure will if it means I can keep my present alimony payments. In any event, thought I better meet with my lawyer just in case something goes wrong."

She looked at the bartender and said, "Ricardo, please put this on our tab, and we'll settle with you at the end of the month, like usual. Okay?"

"*No hay problema, Senora*. See you *manana*." The four women got off their bar stools and headed towards the front door, designer sunglasses firmly in place.

CHAPTER THREE

After the four women had left, Laura and Marty looked at each other, speechless. Marty was the first to speak. "Laura, you're the psychic, what did you make of all that?"

Laura was quiet for several moments, deep in thought, then she picked up her glass of iced tea and rolled it around in her hands. "First of all, I think it points up the main risk when someone has a facelift or some other type of plastic surgery. A lot of people are simply not happy with how it turns out. Secondly, I have a bad feeling about Dr. Ramsey. I can't give you anything specific, but something's swirling around the doctor, and it isn't good. I can't tell you exactly what it is, but something is going to happen and rather soon. Did you pick up on anything when you were in his house?"

"I wish I had some of your psychic powers and then maybe I would have picked up on something, but other than what I told you earlier about his wife, I can't think of anything."

"Marty, I just thought of something, but I have no idea if it means anything. One of our wealthiest insureds came into the office yesterday to talk to Dick. She's inherited her parents' estate and from what she told Dick, and which he shared with me, her parents were long-time antique and art collectors. They'd bought ten acres of land in La Quinta many years ago, when it was pretty cheap.

"Evidently the land had been a citrus orchard. They cleared

enough space to build a home and then more when their daughter was married, so they could live near each other, but each in a very large home. From what she told Dick there were several small houses located on the outskirts of the property for the orchard workers and the people who worked in the houses. Dick mentioned he was going to refer you to handle the appraisal. That's why he wanted to know how far along you were with the Ramsey appraisal."

"Sure, tell him to call me. I'm going to the doctor's office tomorrow morning to appraise the furniture and a few pieces of what's called 'visionary images.' There were several of them in his home, and he told me he has more in his office. They're really rare, so I'm looking forward to it. When I'm finished in his office, I will have seen his entire collection."

"Okay. I have no idea what a visionary image is, and I doubt anyone at the compound does, either. Since we all learn about antiques from you, I won't make you tell me now, but I would like you to tell all of us tonight. Anyway, back to the woman I was talking about. I really don't know what to make of it, but the woman who came in the office to talk to Dick looked a lot like that woman, Brandy, who was sitting at the bar and just left. It was very apparent she'd had a facelift." Laura sat back in her chair and waited for Marty's response.

"I'm not sure what you mean, Laura. Are you saying that because of the facelift your insurance client looked like Brandy? Or are you saying that she just looked similar to Brandy? Since both of them live in the greater Palm Springs area, maybe they're related or even sisters."

"I don't think so. The woman said she was an only child, and there were no other family members other than her husband and their daughter's family. This is a bizarre thought, but do you remember the term 'Stepford Wife?' It actually came from a movie where the wives living in Stepford, Connecticut, were replaced with robots, but now it's kind of loosely referred to as women who look alike or act alike. I have no idea if Brandy and this woman act alike, but they sure do look alike."

"Do you know who your client's plastic surgeon was?" Marty asked.

"No, and there's no way I could ask her, because I'd be insinuating that I thought she'd had a facelift, which is generally the last thing people who have had one want other people to think. They want everyone to believe they took a vacation or went to a spa, and that's why they look so good, not that they spent a bundle of money getting a facelift or some other kind of plastic surgery. That's not even mentioning the apoplectic fit Dick would have if I asked."

"I suppose you're right, but it sure is a coincidence. Maybe plastic surgeons are taught in school that there's an ideal look for a woman who's had plastic surgery."

"Could be, but I have no idea. The only thing I'm sure of at the moment is that I need to get this chimichanga body back to my office before Dick fires me."

"I don't see that happening, Laura," Marty said, taking out her credit card and handing it to the waiter who had appeared with the bill. "I need to visit a couple of antique shops in Palm Springs to see if they have any Shaker items or quilts, since the good doctor had a lot of those, and they looked pretty good against the starkness of the furniture. I'd like to see if I can find some retail values for them, although based on how rare I think the pieces Dr. Ramsey has, that probably isn't going to happen. At least I will have done my due diligence before I start using the Internet and assigning values. I'm glad you could join me for lunch, and for what I'm charging for this appraisal, lunch is on me. See you at home tonight."

CHAPTER FOUR

After she left Armando's restaurant, Marty drove to the Palm Springs Antique Shoppe in downtown Palm Springs and once again thanked the parking fairy who had been sitting on her shoulder when she was trying to find a place to park at Armando's and now here. She easily pulled into an empty space in front of Carl Mitchell's shop.

When she opened the door of the small shop, a bell rang, alerting Carl he had a customer. He walked out of the back room and grinned broadly. "Marty, to what do I owe the pleasure of having you visit my shop?"

"It's probably a longshot, Carl, but I'm wondering if you have any Shaker furniture, baskets, or anything else that's Shaker or even some quilts? If you have any of the visionary art that was popular during that time frame, that would even be better."

"Seriously, Marty? Shaker items are about as rare as Russian Faberge eggs. No, I have absolutely nothing like that, and I sold the last quilt I had yesterday. Sorry, and may I ask why?"

"Yes, I'm finishing up an appraisal on quilts, Shaker furniture, and some other decorative arts of that period, and I need to come up with some comps. Looks like I'll have to resort to the auction records and the Internet."

"Funny you should ask. I have a long-time client that was in the other day. I haven't seen her for a while, and she mentioned she'd gotten married since I'd last seen her, and that her husband collected Shaker pieces. She was curious as to the value of his collection. I told her the same thing I'll tell you. Native American, Southwest Art, jewelry, and even some European antiques I can help with, but Shaker, no, and quilts from that time, only once in a while."

"Carl, you have the best memory in the world. I can't believe there would be two people in the Palm Springs area who collect Shaker items. Do you remember her name, by chance? I wonder if it's the wife of the man whose collection I'm appraising."

"Thanks for the compliment. Of course I remember because she's visited the shop on a number of occasions over the years, but she's only bought a few things, and usually as gifts. Her name is Ashley Ramsey now, although she was Ashley Morrison when I first met her. Her deceased husband was very, very wealthy. I understand he made his money trading on Wall Street and decided to come out here to the Palm Springs area and retire at a relatively young age. Unfortunately, he didn't retire soon enough, because he had a massive heart attack on the golf course one day and left a fortune to Ashley, who is still quite young, like in her mid-30's. She has a lot of money, but she wasn't all that attractive during her first marriage. I guess it's what they say sometimes, that her first husband must have loved her for her personality."

"You say she wasn't all that attractive then. By that do you mean she is now?" Marty asked.

"Well, yes and no. I guess it all depends on how you look at it. When she inherited her husband's fortune, she decided to have some plastic surgery done, specifically a facelift, to enhance her looks. She wasn't ugly by any means, just not all that attractive. The plastic surgeon who operated on her became her husband and changed her looks dramatically. He's the one with the Shaker collection. She's quite attractive now, but she sure doesn't look like the woman I knew before."

"That's weird. I met her the first morning I was at the house to do the appraisal. It never occurred to me she hadn't looked like that originally."

"Ashley told me once that she resented what her husband had done to her face. She said every time she looked in the mirror she felt he must have thought she was unattractive, and that he'd needed to change her to make her acceptable to him. You know, Marty, a lot of the wealthy people in the Palm Springs area come in my shop from time to time and like to talk."

And I know how much you like to listen to gossip and then pass on the more relevant parts, but in this case, I'm glad you do, she thought.

"I know over the years you've built up a very good clientele of the elite of the area, Carl. So, what have you heard?"

He looked around to see if the two customers who were picking up different glass and china pieces to look at the marks on the bottom to make sure they were authentic, were listening to him. He decided they weren't.

"Well, you didn't hear it from me, but the word is, by someone who knows what she's talking about, that the doctor thought Ashley was ugly, at least by his standards, and he told her he could really enhance her looks. What happened is that he completely changed her looks."

Carl sat back, clearly pleased he'd been able to pass on that tidbit of gossip. He waited to see what Marty's reaction was and when he gauged that she'd accepted what he'd told her, he leaned forward and said, "Marty, there's more, and I think it's the best part. My source knew the doctor's second wife left him for their pool boy or rather, man. Anyway, my source says the doctor tried to make Ashley look like his ex-wife, but he botched the surgery. My source also said she's seen a few other women in the Palm Springs area who kind of look like his ex-wife, and every time she sees one she wonders if Dr. Ramsey was the one who operated on her."

"You're kidding, right? I think that's really sick. If that's true, I wonder how the other women feel about how they look. I've never heard of anything like that."

"Me neither, but it sure would make a good movie. I can see it now. All those women would kind of look alike. Yep, bet that would be a hit. Marty, my customer over there is trying to get my attention, so I've got to go. Thanks for stopping by, and if I run into any Shaker furniture or anything else related to Shaker, I'll give you a call."

"Thanks, Carl. Actually, if you run into any other women who look alike, let me know. That is one of the most bizarre things I've ever heard. Glad I've decided not to go under the scalpel."

"Good decision, although you may be the only one in this area who hasn't."

Well, Carl, does that mean you have?

CHAPTER FIVE

On her way home Marty decided to stop by the Hi-Lo Drugstore and give Lucy, the lovable but eccentric photo clerk, the disc of the photographs she'd taken of the items she'd appraised that morning. Usually she sent them to Lucy by way of her computer, but she hadn't seen Lucy since Lucy had gotten a puppy, and Marty was curious how she and her husband were adapting to the new addition to their family.

She opened the door and spotted Lucy behind the counter, looking at photographs with a customer. Marty walked up to the counter and stood a few feet away, so it wouldn't seem like she was listening to their conversation. After a few minutes the customer left, and Lucy turned to Marty.

"Ain't seen you in a coon's age, girl. Got them purty pictures you've been sendin' over fer the last couple of days. Was jes' waitin' fer you to come by and pick 'em up." She reached under the counter and handed Marty a large envelope. "Got any more or was that the last of 'em? Ya' know, I ain't never seen nuthin' like those things. What kinda art stuff are they, anyway?"

"They're called Shaker items. All the things that were in the photos like the furniture, baskets, clocks, artwork, quilts, all of it, is almost two hundred years old. To say those pieces are rare would be the understatement of the year. I've only seen a couple in all of the years that I've been appraising, and to have a collection like this person has is amazing. I want to talk to my client and find out how he became interested in them. He gave me a notebook he said contained information about where he'd gotten them and what he paid for them, but there must be more to it than that."

"One thing kinda leaped out at me. Don't seem like the kind of stuff I'd be comfortable havin' in my home. If you ask me it's pretty bare bones. I mean, sittin' on some piece of plain old wood? My old man wouldn't like that, fer sure. Matter of fact, don't think I would either."

"Speaking of your old man, I want to hear how the two of you are doing with your new puppy. Is the puppy house trained yet?"

Lucy threw back her head and roared with laughter. "Don't know 'bout Killer bein' house trained, but the old man and I sure are puppy trained."

Marty interrupted her. "Lucy, please don't tell me you named that beautiful yellow Lab puppy, Killer. If I were to pick one name that didn't fit a yellow Lab that would be it."

"Well, Marty. Ya' know how it goes. Sometimes ya' jes' gotta roll with the punches, and in this case the punch was the name my old man had always wanted to give to a dog if'n we ever got us one. I couldn't even put an ante in the poker pot, if ya' know what I mean. From the moment we got the little guy, his name was Killer."

"Well, I guess that's that. So, tell me, how is Killer doing, or more importantly, how are you and your husband doing with a puppy?"

"Dang dog has a lot more pull with the old man than I do. Only way I could ever get the old man outta the sack on a weekend mornin' was by cookin' up a load of bacon. He couldn't resist the smell. Well, ya' probably don't wanna hear this, but that dang dog sleeps between us at night. Anyways, when he wants to go outside in the mornin', Killer jes' licks the old man's cheek, and next thing I know the old man's boundin' outta bed and walkin' Killer. Don't that beat all?"

"I'm getting the impression that Killer has definitely wrapped himself around your husband. Are you happy you got him?"

"Can't imagine life without that little love bunny, but I'm kinda gettin' tired of the cookin'."

"Lucy, don't tell me you're cooking special meals for a puppy that doesn't seem to have any health problems."

"No problems I know 'bout. Funny thing. Right after we got him, we was cookin' a steak out on the BBQ. Next thing I know the old man is givin' a big piece of it to Killer. From then on no matter what meat or fish we was cookin', Killer was sittin' 'bout as purty as a dog can sit lookin' up at us with them big brown eyes. Can't say I really cook for him, but will say I sure think about what we're gonna have, so we can share it with him. Killer likes people food."

"I'll bet he does. That's going to be a hard habit to break."

"If'n the old man has anything to do with it, that habit ain't gonna be broke. I mean, it's the least we can do for the little guy. He doesn't ask much in return fer all the love he gives us. Will say my old man has bought every dog toy ever made. He hates to go into Palm Springs fer anything and guess who made a trip yesterday to Palm Springs?

"Yep, ya' guessed it, my old man. Said something 'bout needin' a special light bulb they didn't have at the hardware store here in High Desert. Right. Like the hardware store in Palm Springs has dog toys? Old man came home with a whole bag of 'em. I didn't even ask. He had his head down when he put 'em in Killer's toy box, so I'm guessin' he was a little embarrassed. Yep, our lives have definitely changed, all thanks to you and us takin' care of Duke when ya' was helpin' out John with the food truck at that country music festival where some poor guy went and got hisself murdered."

"Yes, I well remember it. Glad to hear it's working out, Lucy. I probably better get home. John doesn't like it when people are late for dinner."

"Can't say I blame him. Oh, I got a question fer ya'. I saw a woman in one of them photos, yeah I know I ain't supposed to be lookin' at 'em, but kinda figure you and me got an arrangement 'bout that. Anyway, her face looked weird. Seen some women down in the Springs that looked kinda like her. Looked like maybe a bad knife job."

"I'm sorry, Lucy, I have no idea what you're talking about. I don't take pictures of people, just the items I'm appraising."

"Hand me the envelope, honey, and I'll show ya' what I'm talkin' 'bout." She quickly rifled through the photos and picked out one. "Here's the one I'm talkin' 'bout. See the woman in the background? You've heard of a bad hair day? Think she had a bad lift day. Looks like somethin' happened to her face, and I ain't talkin' in a good way." She pushed the photo across the counter to Marty.

Marty look at it and involuntarily said, "Good grief she looks like…" She stopped talking and looked up at Lucy. "Sorry Lucy, I saw someone earlier today who looks a lot like her. I have no idea how she got in this photograph. It looks like a doorway in the background, and she's on the other side. Maybe she was walking down the hall when I took the photograph."

"Could be, but doncha agree with me she looks kinda weird?"

"Lucy, she's my client's wife, and I try to never discuss my clients with anyone, but between you and me, yes, I'd have to agree with you."

"I dunno. Maybe it's cuz all them rich women start lookin' like one another, know what I mean? They all starve themselves so they can look skinnier than they oughtta, wear fancy clothes, have people put paint in their hair, and they call it highlights," she said as she made quote marks with her fingers. She continued, "and they've all had a little work done, although in her case it looks like it was a lot of work, and it sure wasn't by any doctor I'd be wantin' to visit, not that I'm gonna do somethin' like that. Old man tells me he likes me jes' like I am."

"Lucy, I'd have to agree with him," Marty said laughing. "You're an original. I really do need to go. Thanks. Here's my credit card. Why don't you ring me up, and I'll be on my way?"

CHAPTER SIX

Marty knew John didn't like it when the residents of the compound were late to the dinners he prepared almost every night for them. Each of them gave him a monthly stipend in return for the dinners, but all of them still felt guilty about the small amount of the stipend considering how creative and wonderful his food was. Many times they'd raised the subject of increasing the stipend with him, but it always fell on deaf ears. The only nights they had to fend for themselves were when John and Max, who ran the second Red Pony food truck, had a catering event.

When Marty drove in the driveway she was painfully aware that all of the other residents were already there. She quickly got out of her car and hurried through the gate into the central courtyard where the others were all seated around a large picnic table, catching up on the events of the day.

"Hi, guys. Be with you in a minute. I need to put these photos in the house and walk Duke…"

Jeff, her husband of a few months, interrupted her. "I've already done it, Marty, and I'm happy to tell you he is now at peace with the desert. I've been able to convince him that I'm the alpha male."

He was referring to Duke's maddening habit of refusing to put his feet on the desert floor unless he wore the pink booties Marty had bought for him months ago out of frustration. The booties had provided the buffer Duke needed between him and the desert. Les, the very successful and sought-after artist who had been with Laura for many years, had finally broken Duke of his pink bootie habit when he'd walked him a few weeks ago. Les told them that it was very simple. He'd just made Duke aware that he was the alpha male, and Duke was not going to wear booties again. Marty really didn't care how Les had done it, she was just glad she didn't have to put the pink booties on him anymore. She was pretty sure Jeff had taken Les aside, and they'd come up with a scheme so Jeff didn't have to walk a dog wearing pink booties. As a detective with the Palm Spring Police Department, she was sure Jeff was worried about his macho image and reputation. Privately she agreed. Pink booties and a police detective didn't seem to go together.

Marty put the photos she'd picked up at the Hi-Lo Drugstore on the desk in her house and returned to the courtyard. She sat down next to Jeff and took a sip of wine from the glass he handed her. "Laura was just telling us about your lunch and how one of the women at the bar was talking about your doctor client. She told us the woman wasn't happy with the facelift the doctor had done, although Laura thought she looked okay, even if she did have big lips."

"Yes, it was very interesting. A couple of things came up this afternoon that are kind of in that vein." She told them about her conversations with Carl and Lucy. "Let me get the photo of Dr. Ramsey's wife. Evidently I inadvertently took a picture of her, and I'd like all of your opinions as to how she looks. Laura, I'd particularly be interested in what you have to say." Marty stood up and left the table. A few moments later she returned with the photo and passed it around.

"I'll go first," Jeff said. "I think she's attractive, but something seems a little off. She's a little too plastic looking for my taste."

"Thanks, love, that just got you off the hook for having to pay for me to have an expensive operation," Marty said. "If you'd raved about how gorgeous she was, I'd probably have to call a plastic surgeon to get me in on an emergency basis. You just saved us a bunch of money," she said laughing.

Les, Max, and John agreed with Jeff, that the woman in the photo was attractive, but something was off. Laura spent quite a long time looking at the photo. She raised her head and looked at Marty. "Remember when I mentioned the Stepford Wives at lunch? Well, looking at a picture of your client's wife certainly brings it to mind. She looks a lot like that Brandy woman who was sitting at the bar complaining about her facelift. Quite frankly, it kind of creeps me out."

"I agree, Laura. I thought the same thing, but I wanted your opinion. Now I'd like to know if you're getting any psychic vibes from the picture." The residents of the compound and Max looked at Laura expectantly.

She was quiet for several moments, and then she said, "Marty, I told you at lunch I had a bad feeling about the doctor. Seeing the picture of his wife does nothing to allay that feeling, and if anything, it enhances it. Actually, I have a very, very bad feeling about all of this. Something is going to happen, and it's going to happen very soon. I think it's going to involve you and Jeff."

Everyone was quiet while they absorbed what Laura had said. They had learned not to take Laura's predictions lightly, so there was a sense of gloom and foreboding at the table. Jeff was the first to break the silence. "Okay, I'm sensing a dark mood at our table, so I'm going to lift it by sharing some news."

They all turned towards him, and Marty was the first to speak. "Jeff, please, don't make us wait. What is it?"

"Well, you may be looking at the future chief of the detective division of the Palm Springs Police Department. The chief called me in this morning and told me I was the frontrunner for the position. He said he's also considering two other detectives, but right now he's leaning towards yours truly, and he said he'd make a decision very soon." He sat back smiling, clearly pleased.

"Jeff, you never said a word to me about it. You even told me once you weren't sure how the chief felt about you. When did all of this happen?" Marty asked.

"He's kind of hard to read. Actually, I was quite surprised. Anyway, here's what happened. Last week the chief called a special meeting of all the detectives and announced he was taking applications for the position of chief of the detective division. He said it had been vacant for several years, but he felt that it should be reinstated. Anyone who was interested was asked to submit an application. I submitted one a day later. Not only is it a prestigious position, there's a pay increase as well."

Les stood up and walked around the table to where Jeff was sitting. "Let me be the first to congratulate the new chief detective for the Palm Springs Police Department. I have no doubt you'll get the position, and now I can say that I was the first to congratulate you." He put out his hand and Jeff shook it.

Jeff looked at Laura. "I'd be remiss if I didn't ask your take on this, given what I've seen you do the last few months. What are your thoughts?"

"You'll get the position, but, and don't ask me why I'm going to say what I'm going to say, but I'm seeing you running an obstacle course for the next few days."

"Well, I suppose that's a good news and a bad news thing, but at least you see me getting the position," Jeff said. "I suppose it could have been worse."

John motioned to Max, and said, "It's time for us to go perform our miracle in the kitchen. Actually, the miracle has already occurred. I've just been keeping it warm in the oven. Dinner will be served shortly."

"Good timing, John. I see I've got a call from the chief and given what I just told you, I can't afford to let this go to voicemail. I'll be back in a couple of minutes." Jeff walked through the front gate so he could talk to the chief in private.

As it turned out, it was the kind of a call you really don't want to get when you're being considered for a promotion.

CHAPTER SEVEN

"Good evening, Chief. This is Jeff."

"Sorry to interrupt your evening, Jeff, but we've got a new case, a murder. It happened in Palm Desert, but their police chief just called me and asked if we could handle it for them. They're small, and they're overwhelmed right now. I told him you'd be the lead detective on it. It goes without saying that when I make my decision regarding the new chief of the detective division, I'll be looking at how you handle this case. You probably better get over there right away."

"I'm on it, Chief. Who was murdered, and where was the person murdered?"

"He's a plastic surgeon," the chief said. Jeff felt a sinking feeling in the pit of his stomach. *Was this what Laura had been referring to a few minutes earlier?* The chief said, "His name is Keith Ramsey, Dr. Keith Ramsey. Here's his office address where the murder occurred." After hearing the name of the victim, Jeff realized that his sinking feeling was justified. The chief continued, "I want you to notify his wife. I know you've done this kind of a notification before, but try to see to it that she has someone with her when you tell her. That kind of news is never easy on a spouse."

Jeff wrote down the address and said, "That's in the new area of Palm Desert, isn't it? The one with all the fancy shops in it?"

"Yeah, it is. I guess when people pay you big bucks to make them look better, you can afford the high rent district. I'm calling the men who will be working the case with you right now, and I'll tell them to meet you over there. When you've had a chance to figure out what went down, give me a call."

"Will do. How was he murdered?"

"Somebody put a scalpel in his back. Pretty fitting for a guy who makes his living using a scalpel, don't you think?"

"I'd say it's a very interesting choice of a murder weapon," Jeff said. "Wonder if it figures into the murder?"

"Don't know, Detective. That falls into the area of your investigation, but I'm sure you'll figure it out."

"That I will. Talk to you later."

Jeff walked back into the courtyard just as John and Max were serving fried chicken, cole slaw, sourdough biscuits, and red rice. "I'm sorry, John, but the chief just called, and there's been a murder. He's putting me on the case as the lead detective, and I have to leave."

He turned to Laura, "Your psychic abilities were right on, Laura, but what you didn't tell me was that the victim would be the very doctor the woman at the bar was talking about when you and Marty had lunch today. And he's the same doctor who was, and I hate to use that word, since he's now past tense, who was Marty's client."

"Oh, no, Jeff!" Marty exclaimed. "I can't believe it. Can you tell us anything about how he was murdered or when?"

"Marty, here's what the chief told me." He related his recent conversation with the chief to them. "That's all I know. I'm on my way to the murder scene. I'll try and call you later tonight. If you don't hear from me, go to bed, and I'll talk to you in the morning."

"Jeff, one thing before you leave. I'm supposed to go to Dr. Ramsey's office tomorrow morning to complete my appraisal. I wonder if that's even going to be possible."

"I'll put your name down as someone who's allowed to have access to his office which is now a crime scene. His staff is going to have to go in and cancel his appointments and surgeries. I have no idea if he has a partner or anything else at this point. I really need to leave. See you all tomorrow." Jeff turned to go into the house and get his gun before be left.

The remaining residents and Max were quiet after he left, then Marty spoke. "I think I'm in shock. I only met the doctor a couple of times, and while he wasn't a particularly warm fuzzy type of person, I can't believe someone would want to murder him." She turned to Laura and said, "You probably better call Dick and tell him what's happened. I don't know whether to submit the appraisal report as an insurance appraisal or as a probate appraisal, so I'd like you ask him what he wants me to do."

"You're right. I'll call him right now. My phone's in the house. Back in a few minutes," Laura said as she stood up.

When she returned, she said, "Dick wants you to complete the report. He's going to call the doctor's lawyer in the morning and find out how he wants you to proceed with the appraisal, but he said it would probably be an appraisal for probate. I don't know if that changes the values you'll place on the items, but I think you told me the pieces are quite unique and that you needed to do some research on the Internet. Does that help?"

"It helps, but I'm dreading going into the place where he was murdered. Just the thought of it makes me uncomfortable. I'm really curious to see what Jeff finds out."

"Well, everybody, look at it this way. We have a front row center seat at a story which will probably be on all the news reports tonight as well as the lead headline in tomorrow's paper," Les said. "I'm sorry about your client, Marty, but John, I can't help myself. For some perverted reason, all this talk of death makes me hungry. Maybe it's because I'm alive. I'm sure some shrink would have a wonderful time trying to figure that out, but I have to tell you that the chicken looks delicious. I'm going to be the first to help myself," Les said.

"Please, everybody, take some food. Marty, that includes you," John said. "You'll need your strength for what you might find tomorrow."

"Great thought, John, thanks," she said dryly as she took a little of everything. After her first bite of chicken she looked up and said, "John, this is probably the best fried chicken I've ever had, and coming from the Midwest, I'm definitely no stranger to it. My compliments to the chef."

"Thanks. Try the red rice, Marty. I think it goes perfectly with the chicken. I'd love all of your thoughts on it."

"John, what do you do? Spend every minute you're not cooking watching television food shows and reading cookbooks? The rice is perfect with the chicken. As usual, you've outdone yourself," Les said.

"Thanks, all. As they say in Italy, mangia, mangia, or eat up!"

CHAPTER EIGHT

When Marty woke up the following morning, Jeff still hadn't returned. She made a cup of coffee, walked Duke, and called Jeff. "Sorry to bother you, sweetheart, but I was concerned when I got up and saw that you hadn't come home last night. I want to touch base with you before I go to Dr. Ramsey's office. What's happening, and is there anything I should know?"

"Not really. The crime scene was a mess. His medical partner was the one who found him and he's devastated, which isn't surprising. I had to notify his staff and his wife, as well as oversee the crime scene investigation. Then I had to go to my office and write up the reports. I didn't even get to the station until 4:00 a.m. To say I'm exhausted would be the understatement of the year. I'm running on nothing but coffee and donuts right about now. I should be home in an hour or so. When are you leaving?"

"Probably about the time you'll be getting home. I won't even bother to make the bed, because I'm assuming you'll just fall into it."

"That's exactly what I plan on doing. I just hope I can sleep given the gallons of coffee I've consumed over the last few hours. If I don't see you this morning, I'll catch up with you later. I'm going to try and grab a couple of hours of sleep, but I need to get this investigation going. As I've told you before, the first few hours are always the most critical when it comes to trying to solve a murder case."

"Anything you can tell me at this point?" Marty asked.

"His partner had neglected to look at the surgery schedule for today and wanted to see what time his first one was scheduled for. He couldn't get his home computer to work, so he went to his office to see if he could pull it up there. Instead, he found a scalpel in Dr. Ramsey's back. He was sitting in front of his computer, and it was on. That's about the gist of it. Naturally Dr. Ramsey's computer is being checked for anything that might help us. My team gathered about thirty bags of DNA evidence. Other than that, I'm waiting for the DNA and fingerprint tests to come back. Although I briefly talked to the doctor's staff last night, I need to interview each of them at length to see if they can come up with any persons of interest. Right now I don't have one, which is not a good way to start an investigation.

"Jeff, I'm assuming you and your team went through his desk and everything else last night. I just want to make sure it's okay for me to touch things when I do the appraisal this morning. It's almost impossible to conduct one without doing that."

"Yeah, Marty, we were pretty thorough. All the evidence we felt was relevant has been removed from the office, but we didn't take any of the furniture in his office, the quilts, or the artwork that was on the walls."

"Try and get some sleep, Jeff. I'm sure when you're rested, your mind will kick into high gear, and you'll find the murderer."

"Thanks, love. I wish I shared your optimism. The thing that's bothering me is I know the chief is watching every step I'm taking. If I can't solve this case, it's a pretty safe bet to assume I won't be the one who will be leading the detective division in the future."

"Well, I hate to say it, but you may have a point. I'd like to take Laura with me to Dr. Ramsey's office this morning and see if she can get a sense of anything, but I don't think I could come up with a reason for her to be there other than she could pretend to be my assistant."

"Nice idea, Marty, but I don't think Dick would appreciate you borrowing Laura for the morning. He's been very good to you, and you sure don't want to jeopardize your standing with him."

"You're probably right, but I wouldn't mind seeing what her read on the situation at the office is. Anyway, I'll see you tonight. I love you, and I worry about you."

"Don't waste your time worrying about me. I'd rather you spent it wishing me luck in finding out who murdered Dr. Ramsey."

"Okay, I wish you luck in finding out who murdered the doctor. Bye."

As soon as she ended the call, she walked next door to Laura's house. The door was ajar, and she said in a loud voice, "Laura, it's me. Can I come in?"

"Sure. I was just getting ready to go outside and check on the weather to see what I should wear to work today. Although we live in the high desert, which is supposed to be somewhat cool this time of year, I always like to do a personal morning assessment. The weather people are good, but I think I trust my own instincts more than all their fancy equipment."

"I know what you mean. Laura, I have a favor to ask. It seems to me that you told me once that the insurance company gives each employee a couple of days a year which they call personal days, days they can take care of personal business. I was wondering if you've taken your personal days this year."

Laura had been buttoning her blouse when Marty had come in, and at her question, she paused. "The answer is no, but why do you ask?"

"Well," Marty said, looking around the room and avoiding Laura's eyes, "I just talked to Jeff. He and his investigative team collected a lot of DNA evidence and fingerprints at the doctor's office when they were there." She began to speak hurriedly, "Like I said last night,

I have to go there this morning to finish my appraisal, and I was thinking, with your psychic ability, maybe you could pick up something that wasn't apparent to Jeff's team." She turned back to Laura with a pleading look in her eyes.

"Wait a minute, Sis. I'm in the middle of getting dressed to go to my job, which is a very high-paying and prestigious job with a blue-chip insurance company, and you want me, on no notice, to call in and use a day reserved for personal business to go with you to an appraisal at a dead doctor's office. Is that what you're saying?"

"When you put it that way, Laura, it sounds like I'm really pushing the boundaries of our sisterly relationship. Never mind, maybe I can find something on my own." She dejectedly turned to leave.

"Where do you think you're going? I didn't say I wouldn't do it, Marty. I just wanted to make sure that when I want you to do something for me, you'll jump at whatever it is. Actually, I kind of remember how you used to manipulate me when we were kids, and I was always the one who got caught by mom and dad when we did something wrong. You still know how to manipulate me. Sure, I'll call in and tell Dick I'm taking a personal day."

"Oh, Laura, thank you. I just know you'll come up with something. Actually, you don't need to take a full day. The appraisal isn't going to last more than a couple of hours, three at tops. You'll be back in the office in time for lunch."

"You owe me, and I may just collect with another chimichanga at Armando's. After we raved about them to John last night, I just hope he can make one that's close to being as good as theirs. Let me change clothes. I'm not exactly sure what's appropriate for helping with an appraisal in a place where a murder took place, but I don't think I should wear a business suit. We can take separate cars, because I do have to go to the office when we're finished. When do you want to leave?"

"In about forty-five minutes. I need to get dressed, and I want to eat something. See you in a few."

CHAPTER NINE

Marty walked into Dr. Ramsey's suite of offices, followed by Laura who was carrying Marty's large photography bag. Marty had her tape recorder, tape measure, and everything else she needed for the appraisal in a brown leather briefcase that had become faded with use.

She walked over to the reception desk and said, "Good morning. I'm Marty Morgan-Combs. I'm the appraiser Dr. Ramsey hired to do his collection of Shaker furniture, quilts, and art. I am so sorry to hear of his death, and I realize this isn't a good time to be opening up your office to strangers, but the insurance company wants me to complete my report as soon as possible. They told me they'll need it even though their insured is now deceased. I've brought my assistant, Laura, with me."

The older woman sitting behind the front counter said, "I'm Sybil West, Dr. Ramsey's administrative assistant. He told me yesterday that you would be coming in this morning and he asked me to give you full access to his office. I'm sure you can understand that all of us who have worked for the doctor are in a state of shock. You can enter his office by going down the hall. It's the last door on the left," she said.

"Please let me know if you need anything. I'd come with you, but right now I'm pretty involved in putting out fires. Everyone wants Dr. Thurman, he was Dr. Ramsey's associate, to do their procedure, since we're having to cancel all of Dr. Ramsey's appointments and scheduled surgeries. In addition to Dr. Thurman's regular schedule, this is rapidly becoming a nightmare. Sorry to sound so negative, but I've only been here one hour, and I think this very well may be the longest day I've ever spent in the office."

"I can only imagine what you're dealing with," Marty said. "I'm sure we won't need anything. We'll check with you before we leave."

She turned to go and heard Sybil say, "I forgot to tell you that Dr. Ramsey had a room he used as a conference room behind his office. He mentored a lot of interns, and there's a big conference table in there. That room has some pieces from his collection in it as well."

"Thanks. I'm sure we won't have any problems." She and Laura walked down the hall and opened the door to Dr. Ramsey's office. Laura entered the room and gasped. "I've never seen any furniture like this. It's so simple and yet elegant. I know absolutely nothing about Shaker things. What makes them so special and rare? As I recall the Shaker settlements were in the Eastern United States, but that's about all I know."

"Yes, they were a religious sect that preached simplicity. They didn't believe in using ornamental additions like inlays or carvings, but rather relied on drawer arrangements that weren't the same size and things of that nature to create their art. The furniture was usually made of cherry, maple, or pine. Often it was stained, like those pieces over there," Marty said, gesturing to a table and chairs on the far side of the room.

"Marty, they're all beautiful, but the chairs sure don't make me feel like I want to sit down and relax in one of them. I have to tell you they look both forbidding and uncomfortable."

"Not surprising when you consider the Shakers were completely self-sufficient and very much opposed to anything that seemed to be prideful or egotistical."

"That artwork is poles apart from what Les paints," Laura said in reference to Les' larger-than-life modernistic paintings.

"It certainly is. Their life was couched in religiosity, and their artwork reflected that. The tree of life is one of the oldest symbols around, and it denotes strength, growth, and connectedness. The Shakers were quite taken with this image because they thought it depicted the branches reaching towards heaven. And, as I'm sure you know, they were only one of many different groups that extensively used that symbol. I find it interesting that all of the quilts Dr. Ramsey collected primarily had that motif."

"Thanks for the lesson, Sis, now give me my marching orders."

"Laura, you've helped me with appraisals a couple of times before. If you could measure the pieces while I photograph them and dictate the information about them, that would really be helpful. I'd also like you to take the quilts and artwork off the walls and check the backs. Often people put information about them on the reverse side, such as where they got the piece, what they paid for it, or who the artist was. Let's get started."

Laura took the measurements of the pieces while Marty photographed them and dictated the pertinent information about them to use in her research. When she had determined the value of each one, she would dictate all of the information into a report to be given to the woman who typed up her reports.

"That's it, Laura," Marty said as she hung the last piece of artwork back on the wall. "Have you picked up anything? Get any vibes?"

"Not about the pieces, but his desk has been talking to me ever since I entered the room. Would it be all right with you if I went through it?"

"That's fine. As a matter of fact, I was going to do the same. It's been my experience that people often stick something in their desk or a drawer and don't realize it has value. Usually it's something small, and for some reason human nature tends to overlook small things."

"With the exception of jewelry," Laura replied.

"That's true, but we're not appraising jewelry. Go ahead and sit down. Believe me, I'd love it if you could find something. I'm going to look through the drawers that are in the furniture. Maybe we'll get lucky."

They were both quiet for several moments. Laura was the first to speak, "Marty, I found something, but I don't think it has anything to do with his collection."

Marty walked over to the desk where Laura was sitting and said, "What did you find?"

She held up a photograph of a woman and said, "Look like anyone you know?"

Marty took the photograph and examined it. She looked at Laura and said, "I think my eyes are playing tricks on me. This woman looks a lot like Brandy, the woman we saw at Armando's yesterday, and she also looks like the woman in the photograph I inadvertently took of Dr. Ramsey's wife."

"Yes, but she looks a whole lot better than they do. They're kind of poor imitations of this woman. I wonder who she is."

"I have no idea. Where did you find it? I'm surprised Jeff's crime scene investigation team didn't see it, although maybe they did, and didn't think it was important."

"I don't think they found it. This was kind of one of those psychic things that happens to me. There was a list of telephone numbers taped to the bottom of this drawer," Laura said, pointing to one of the drawers. "And for whatever reason, I felt compelled to pull the tape away. I kept getting a feeling there was something very important underneath the list. That's where I found the photograph. I'm sure Jeff's team wouldn't have thought to do that, because the list of phone numbers was securely taped to the drawer."

"I'm really curious about who this woman is," Marty said. "I have no idea if it has any relevance to Dr. Ramsey's death, but the fact the woman looks so much like the other two women seems very odd."

"I agree. What are you going to do with it?"

"I think I'll ask Sybil, the office manager out front, if she has any idea who it is. Jeff specifically told me that his team was finished with the office, so I don't think it would be a problem if I asked her," Marty said.

"Go for it. Maybe she can give you some additional information about the woman. I'm going to let you handle it. Dick was very gracious about me taking the morning off, but I don't want to push it. Since it looks like we're finished here, I'm going back to the office. See you tonight."

"Thanks, Laura, I really appreciate you doing this for me. I owe you," Marty said as she put away her appraisal equipment. "Enjoy your afternoon."

CHAPTER TEN

After Laura left, Marty gathered up her appraisal gear and walked down the hall to the reception area. Sybil was just ending a call. "Well, were you able to finish your appraisal?" she asked.

"Yes, thank you. Dr. Ramsey had some beautiful pieces. I wonder what's going to happen to his collection?"

"I have no idea. I imagine his wife will get everything, but I don't know that for a fact," she said with a frown on her face.

Hmmmm, that's interesting, Marty thought. *I don't have Laura's psychic powers, but I sure get the feeling there's no love lost there.* An idea popped into her mind. An idea that might mean she could get some information to help Jeff with his investigation.

"Sybil, this is totally spur of the moment, but I'm starving. You must be exhausted from juggling so many balls this morning. Can you take a little time off to join me for lunch? I'm craving some Mexican food, and my favorite place, Armando's, is just down the street."

Sybil looked at her computer for a moment and then said, "I'd like that. I really need a break, and at least I've been able to cancel the doctor's appointments and surgeries for the rest of the day, although I still have a lot of calls to make. Let me tell Denise I'm leaving. I'll just be a minute."

She got up from her desk and walked into a back office which Marty assumed was where the patient's billing information and medical records were kept, since she didn't see any files in the front office, other than the ones Sybil had on her desk. Sybil returned a few moments later with her purse slung over her shoulder.

When they walked into Armando's, Marty experienced a feeling of déjà vu. The only table that was unoccupied was the exact one she and Laura had sat at when they'd had lunch there the day before. The bartender smiled at her and waved her over to it.

After they were seated, Marty asked, "Since the restaurant is so close to your office, do you come here often?"

"I'm usually here about once a week. I think they have a pretty regular lunchtime group that eats here. Actually, I see several people who have been patients over the years."

While they were looking at their menus, Marty asked, "How long have you worked for Dr. Ramsey?"

"I've been with him since he took over his father's practice, which was about twenty years ago. Originally, he was the only doctor in the office, but the practice became so successful he had to bring in another surgeon. Dr. Thurman has been with him for about five years."

"I've not met him. I imagine Dr. Ramsey's death is going to change quite a few things at your office." She looked up from her menu and saw the tears in Sybil's eyes. "I didn't mean to sound insensitive," she said as she reached out and covered Sybil's hand with hers. "I'm sure this is a horrible time for you and the staff."

"It is. None of them have been with the doctor as long as I have. I don't know what to expect. I can't imagine not having Dr. Ramsey in my life. I've devoted everything to him, and now…"

Marty sensed there was more to her grief than would be expected from an employee. The waiter appeared and took their orders, iced tea and tacos for both of them.

Sybil continued, "He used me as a sounding board for so many things, business, personal..." She stopped talking and dabbed at her eyes with a handkerchief she'd taken out of her purse. "He started his practice right after he divorced his first wife, and I consoled him then. He was single for several years, and then he met Lisbeth. They had two children, and I'm actually the godmother for his daughter. They were married for ten years, and then Lisbeth decided she was in love with their pool man. She filed for divorce and got custody of their two children, Matt and Dani. The whole thing devastated Keith."

"I can imagine it would. What was his wife like?"

"She was beautiful. I always wondered if that's one of the reasons he fell in love with her. Being a plastic surgeon, he appreciated beauty, and she was probably the most beautiful woman I've ever seen. I've often wondered..." she stopped talking and took a sip from the glass of iced tea the waiter had put in front of her.

"You were saying," Marty prodded.

"Oh, it's nothing. Just an opinion. It really isn't important. I'm babbling as it is. Chalk it up to exhaustion and grief. I didn't get much sleep last night."

"Sybil, my husband is a Palm Springs police officer, and he's the lead detective investigating the murder of Dr. Ramsey. The one thing I've learned from being with him is that everything is important. Maybe what you have to say is important and could help him solve the case."

Sybil appeared to be deep in thought. She looked around the room to see if anyone nearby was listening and then leaned in close towards Marty. "This is just my opinion, and I'm sure it means nothing, and I probably shouldn't even say it, but I suppose it doesn't matter now. I don't think Keith ever got over Lisbeth. Yes, he remarried, but I think it was strictly a marriage of convenience. Ashley had a lot money, and Keith had the opportunity to take a drab-looking woman and make her attractive. I really never thought there was much love lost on either of their parts."

Marty took a bite of the taco the waiter had served her and then said, "That doesn't seem unusual, and I don't see how that could have anything to do with the case, unless she resented the fact that she looked better, although that seems unlikely."

"Well," Sybil said, "that's not exactly true. She looks better than she did, but once I heard her screaming at him over the phone that she didn't look anything like she used to." She sat back as if Marty should understand what she was saying.

"I'm sorry, Sybil, what you just said confuses me. Wouldn't someone want to look better, and not like they used to look if they had plastic surgery?"

"Yes and no. Keith used to take the women he performed surgery on and make them beautiful, but there were still elements in their looks that made each of them unique. If you use my name, I'll deny this, but a couple of years after Lisbeth left him, it seemed that many of the women he did facelifts on began to look a bit alike. I always thought he was trying to recreate Lisbeth and couldn't."

"Wow. I don't know anything about plastic surgeons and ethics, but that seems to border on unethical. Were any of the women upset about what he'd done to their faces? Were there a lot of them?"

"No, not that many. I think he used a certain criterion for women he was going to do it on. Take a look at the woman sitting over there at the bar. Her name's Brandy. Her hairstylist is considered to be the best in Palm Springs, and he's the one who referred her to Dr. Ramsey. She looks a lot like Lisbeth, but just not spot on. Actually, she's pretty upset about how she looks. She's called the office several times to complain, and she even threatened to sue him."

Marty looked at the woman named Brandy, the woman she'd seen in Armando's the day before. "She may be upset about how she looks, Sybil, but I sure do like her hairstyle. Do you know the name of her hairdresser?" Marty thought she might make an appointment with him and see what he had to say about Brandy.

"It's Brett Joseph, but I want to warn you, he's not cheap. He's referred a lot of woman to Dr. Ramsey over the years. I always bought an expensive Christmas present for him from Keith. Dr. Ramsey really appreciated the referrals, because anyone referred by Brett could well afford Keith's fee. Even Dr. Thurman went to Brett."

"Well, I imagine he could well afford to go there, what with the cost of plastic surgery."

"He could, but then again he might not be able to buy that big yacht he's always talking about. Maybe he'll put that down in his diary."

"I'm afraid you lost me, Sybil. I'm gathering he wants to buy a big yacht, but what is the reference to his diary?"

"Dr. Thurman has a boat he keeps in Newport Beach and most weekends he drives over to the coast and spends time on it. For the last year he's been saying he probably needs to up his plastic surgery fees, so he can afford to buy a boat he wants that's for sale in Newport Harbor. It's pretty big. I think he said it was big enough that if he bought it he could cruise the world when he retired."

"That I can understand, but a diary? I can't imagine a doctor keeping a diary. Is it notes about his patients?"

"I don't know. I've never seen what's in it. He's very secretive about it, but all of us who work there have seen him write in it at one time or another. We all just referred to it as his diary. Maybe it's a habit that's left over from his childhood. I'm sorry. I know I'm babbling, and there was absolutely no reason for me to bring that up."

"No problem, Sybil. Considering everything you're been dealing with, I'm impressed you can walk, talk, and eat. I do have a question for you. You mentioned Dr. Ramsey's wife and this woman, Brandy. Were there others over the years who were upset with the way the doctor's surgeries turned out?" Marty asked with an innocent look on her face, as she took a sip of her iced tea.

"Not really, no, wait. I take that back. Not too long ago the doctor did a facelift on a woman named Missy Donaldson. I don't think she was all that upset about how she looked, but her husband was furious. He actually came to the office and accused Dr. Ramsey of taking away the woman he loved and making her face into someone else's."

"Would that face have resembled his second wife?"

"Yes, but again, not exactly. There was a strong resemblance, but Lisbeth was always the beauty. The other women paled by comparison." She looked at her watch. "I'm sorry I'm such bad company, and I've said way more than I should have. Usually I never say a word about the doctors or our patients, but I'm just..."

"Sybil, you don't need to explain. I understand, and I wish you the best of luck. Hopefully, as bad as this seems now, you can move on, and I suppose the only bright light is that you'll have your life back."

At that, Sybil started sobbing hard enough that several nearby diners looked in their direction. "You don't understand. I loved Keith. I've loved him for twenty years, and all he did was go from one woman to another and this last wife is the worst. At least she won't be able to have him anymore. I really must go," she said between sobs. She put several bills on the table. "Here's for lunch. Maybe we'll see each other again." She stood up and hurriedly left the restaurant in a rush, not caring who saw that she was crying.

When the waiter brought the bill over a few minutes later, Marty gave him the money Sybil had left on the table as well as some of her own. She sat at the table after he'd left for a few minutes, deciding what to do next. She was sure the photograph Laura had found was that of Dr. Ramsey's second wife, Lisbeth, the love of his life, but she felt she needed confirmation of her suspicions that Lisbeth was the woman in the photograph.

Because Sybil left the restaurant so abruptly, she hadn't had time to ask her if she could identify the woman. She decided to pay another visit to Carl. He seemed to know anyone and everyone who was someone in the Palm Springs area. She was sure he could help her.

CHAPTER ELEVEN

When Marty opened the door of Carl's antique shop, she saw him examining a box of what appeared to be small paperweights. He looked up and said, "Seriously, Marty? Two visits in two days? Unless I'm mistaken, this is some kind of a record. Usually I only see you every couple of months. I'm assuming you want some more information. Did you find something else in your appraisal you need my advice on?"

"I wish it was that easy, Carl. I don't know if you've seen the television news today or read The Desert Sun, but Dr. Ramsey was murdered last night, and..."

Carl interrupted her, a shocked look on his suntanned face. "You're kidding! I can't believe it. I've been involved in an appraisal the last few days, and between researching it, and working here, I haven't had time to look at television or read anything. What happened?"

Marty filled him in on what she knew, excluding what she'd learned during her recent lunch with Sybil. "Carl, when I was appraising the items in the doctor's office this morning, I found this photograph. Do you recognize the person in it?"

He took it from her and looked at it for a long time. "Marty, this is really weird. It looks a lot like Ashley Ramsey, but it's not. I've had several clients in the last few years who also looked like this woman. I know I've seen this woman or a picture of her. Give me a minute." Again, he looked at it and then abruptly walked into the back room where his office was located.

When he returned he was holding a scrapbook. "Don't judge me, Marty, because I know it's not all that masculine," he said defensively, "but when I'm involved in something that makes the papers, I like to clip the article and save it. When my mother comes to visit, she loves to know what I've been doing during the year. I knew I'd seen that woman before, but it just took me a minute to identify her. Look, here she is."

He handed the scrapbook to Marty and pointed to a newspaper article with an accompanying photograph of a woman standing next to Carl. Several other women flanked them. Marty quickly read the article and looked up at Carl.

"So, you were donating your appraisal services for the evening at a fundraising event for the hospital? The woman standing next to you looks exactly like the woman in the photograph I showed you."

"Yes I was, but look closer, Marty. I was pretty sure I knew who it was after I thought about it for a moment, but I wanted to be sure before I told you. It's Lisbeth Ramsey, Dr. Ramsey's ex-wife. She divorced him, and as I'm pretty sure I told you, it was quite the scandal in Palm Springs. I haven't seen or heard anything about her since, but everyone was talking about it at the time. I never associated her looks with those of Ashley and several other of my clients, but there is an eerie resemblance. What do you think that's all about?"

"Carl, I honestly have no idea what it's about, or if it even figures into his murder, but it sure is strange that several women would just happen to look like his ex-wife. That's kind of bizarre and definitely something Jeff needs to know about."

"I take it from that statement your husband is involved in this case. No wonder you're trying to help."

"Carl, it's more than that. Jeff is being considered for the position of head detective of the Palm Springs Police Department. He really needs to solve this case as soon as possible to show the chief that he's the most qualified person for the position. I have no idea what he'll do with this information, but perhaps it has some relevance to the case. Anyway, I won't take up any more of your time, but thanks for verifying what I sort of suspected."

"Marty, would you answer something for me?"

"Sure, Carl, what is it?"

"Is your sister, Laura, involved in this case?"

"Why do you ask?"

"Because I still have nightmares about the time you called me in to help with an appraisal, and we couldn't find a ring the decedent's son was sure his mother had. When your sister walked in with that big knife, slit open the wig stand, and took out that big rock, I couldn't believe what I was seeing. I was so frightened I thought I was going to pass out. Now I know she's a psychic, but I still find it hard to believe what she did that day."

"So do I, Carl, and in answer to your question, yes, she is helping me."

"Maybe I'm the psychic one. I just knew she was involved, and if she is, I think I'll bow out. Seeing her in action once was enough for me," he said with a mock shiver.

"I'll be sure and give your best to her," Marty said laughing as she walked out the door.

CHAPTER TWELVE

When Marty returned to the compound where she and Jeff lived, she pulled into the driveway and saw Duke lying in his usual position next to the gate. Whenever she left the compound she knew when she returned he'd be waiting for her. She grinned when she got out of the car and said, "Duke, guess what? I returned safe and sound, just like I always do, so you can relax. Come on, let's go for a walk. You can probably use one."

Now that Les had convinced Duke he could actually put his feet on the desert floor without wearing his pink booties, it was a lot easier to walk him. When they were through, Marty got her appraisal gear out of the trunk of her car and walked through the gate into the compound courtyard. It was late afternoon, but too early for the residents to meet to catch up on the day's activities and share dinner, which was fine with Marty, because she had a number of things she needed to do. Her head was spinning with everything she'd learned today. The first thing on her to-do list was to make a hair appointment with Brandy's hairstylist, Brett Joseph.

Marty changed into a pair of jeans, a tank top, and a vintage pink and rose colored kimono top that she tied at her waist. Even though she didn't sew and didn't consider herself to be the least bit creative, she loved the feel and texture of fabrics. This was a new look for her, and she hoped Jeff would like it.

She went in the kitchen to get a glass of iced tea, and when she walked by her office, she noticed the red light blinking on her answer machine, indicating she had a message. A moment later she sat down at her desk and listened to it.

"I'm calling for Marty Morgan-Combs," the female voice said. "This is Dr. Ramsey's wife, Ashley Ramsey. We met briefly the other day. I know you've been conducting an appraisal of my husband's collection of Shaker furniture, art, and quilts. I was wondering if you could come to my home tomorrow. I'd like to discuss the appraisal with you. Please call me when you get this message. My number is …"

Well, that's weird, Marty thought. *I wonder what she wants.*

She dialed the number Ashley had left and a moment later a voice answered. "Ramsey residence. May I help you?"

"Yes, this is Marty Morgan-Combs. I'm returning Ashley Ramsey's call. May I speak with her?"

"Just a moment," the voice said. "I'll see if she's available."

Marty felt like screaming, "She's the one who called me, for Pete's sake and wanted me to call her. Of course she's available."

A few moments later a voice said, "Hello, Marty. Thanks for returning my call. I'd like to talk to you tomorrow if you have the time. Could you come to the house? Given everything that's happened, I really don't feel up to going out yet."

"I understand, and I'd be happy to. What's a good time for you? My schedule for tomorrow is very flexible."

"I'd like to get this over with. Say, 10:00 tomorrow morning?"

"That would be fine, Mrs. Ramsay. I'll see you then."

Marty ended the call and held the phone in her hand for a

moment. *I wonder why she wants to see me. I better call Dick and get his advice on the values I need to use in the report. Insurance and probate values are usually quite different.*

She dialed the number for the insurance company and asked to speak with him. A moment later she recognized Laura's voice. "Hi, Sis. What are you doing answering Dick's phone? I thought you were some high-level executive, and they don't usually answer their own phones," she said in a teasing tone.

"Good afternoon to you, too," Laura responded. "I'm answering Dick's phone because I'm in his office. His administrative assistant became ill and had to go home, and to answer your question, neither one of us usually answers our phone. I'm assuming you want to speak with Dick."

"That would be the right assumption."

"He's finishing up with a client, Marty. It'll be just a moment."

Evidently Laura had put her hand over the receiver, since Marty could faintly hear Laura telling Dick she was on the phone, then she heard Dick say, "Good afternoon, Marty. What can I do for you?"

"Dr. Ramsey's wife called me, and I'm going to meet with her tomorrow morning. She said it was about the appraisal. Have you talked to her or is there something I should know?"

"No, I haven't talked to her, but her lawyer called me a little while ago and wondered if there had been an appraisal done of the doctor's collection. Evidently Dr. Ramsey had told him that it was quite valuable. Since Dr. Ramsey had a trust, there's no need for a probate appraisal. Just prepare it as you normally would for a regular insurance appraisal. Even though he's deceased, it still needs to be insured."

"Okay. Since I have no idea what she wants to talk to me about, I wanted to be sure in my mind what you wanted me to do before I met with her."

"There may be more to it than that, Marty. When I asked the lawyer if Mrs. Ramsey would be inheriting his estate, he was very vague. I know Dr. Ramsey has a son and a daughter by a prior marriage. If the present Mrs. Ramsey thinks she's going to inherit it all, she may be in for a surprise. The lawyer didn't say that directly to me, but I just had a sense there was more involved with the estate than just putting a value on it."

"Well, if I find out anything after I talk to her, I'll let you know."

"Marty, when do you think you can have the appraisal ready for the attorney?"

"It's going to take me a little while, Dick. Those items are really unique. I know I'm going to have to spend a lot of time looking at auction sale records for comparable pieces. I should probably have it completed within, say, two to three weeks."

"I don't think that will be a problem. By the way, your client is now the estate, not Dr. Ramsey, so send your bill to the attorney. I'll email you with his information."

"Dick, why am I getting the feeling this could get ugly?"

"Probably because I share the same feeling. Either way, give me a call tomorrow after your meeting with the widow. I've only met her once, but she sure didn't leave me with the feeling my life wouldn't be complete unless I saw her again. Good luck."

"Swell, that's just what I needed to hear. Talk to you tomorrow."

Marty spent the next few minutes looking up the telephone number for Brett Joseph's salon. When she Googled his name, the name of his salon came up. It was very simply named "Brett." She called the number after looking at several photographs that had been put up on the salon's website. Having appraised so many offices and homes over the years, whenever there was artwork in niches with special lighting on them, she knew whatever they sold there was going to be expensive. She noticed that no price menu for the salon's services was posted on the website. Marty decided she better take a couple of credit cards with her when she went to her appointment if she was lucky enough to get one.

"Brett's Salon," the female voice said in a heavy French accent. "May I help you?"

"Yes, I'd like to make an appointment with Brett for a cut and possibly adding some highlights."

"Have you been to the salon before?"

"No, but he came highly recommended. When do you have an opening?" Marty asked, certain that she'd made a mistake in calling. From the imperious tone of voice the receptionist had, she figured there was no way the high and mighty Brett would have an opening for the next month or two. She'd about decided to cancel her request, since the murder investigation would have been solved long before then.

"I know this is very short notice, but a woman just called and cancelled her standing monthly appointment for tomorrow afternoon, because she's ill," the snooty voice said. "Is there any chance you could come then? Brett doesn't like it when he has free time during his day, and as in demand as he is, that's pretty rare."

"Yes, that would be wonderful. What time would you like me there?"

"We like our clients to arrive here about fifteen minutes before their appointments, so they can put on a gown and get comfortable. His assistant will wash your hair before he sees you. Your appointment will be at 1:00, so be here at 12:45. Come with a clear idea of what you want him to do, because he doesn't like to waste time while a client tries to make up her mind about what she wants done."

"Thank you, and I'll see you then," Marty said, wondering what this person Brett would be like. Based on her phone call with his receptionist and the photographs she'd seen of the salon, she pictured Brett as being a very imposing tall French man with icy blue eyes and a condescending manner. She sincerely hoped if she was going to spend the kind of money she figured it was going to cost, that she was wrong.

CHAPTER THIRTEEN

One by one, the residents of the compound drifted into the courtyard after they'd changed out of their work clothes, returned phone calls, and did whatever else needed to be done before they could take time to relax and enjoy one of John's fabulous dinners.

When everyone was seated around the big outdoor table, Laura turned to Marty and said, "Did you find out who the woman was in the photograph I found in the doctor's office?"

"You found a photograph in his office?" Jeff asked as he turned to her. When he'd arrived at the compound, he'd told the others he had to go back to work after dinner, but that he needed a break, so he'd come home for dinner before his meeting at eight that evening with his investigative team.

"Well, your wife was very persuasive about me going to the doctor's office with her this morning," Laura said. "She wanted to know if I'd pretend to be her assistant, but what she really wanted to know was if I could pick up any psychic vibes while I was there."

"And did you?" Jeff asked.

"Well, yes and no. I did find a photograph of a woman underneath a telephone list in his desk…"

Jeff interrupted her. "What are you talking about? My people carefully inspected that desk and everything else in the room."

Laura told him she'd had a feeling about the telephone list that was taped to the bottom of one of the drawers, and when she'd lifted the paper up, she'd found a photograph beneath it.

"I can't believe you found something," Jeff said. "You know with each of my cases you get involved in, you're making me believe more and more in this psychic stuff. Okay, I'll bite. What did the photograph show?"

"It was of a woman, quite a beautiful woman, as a matter of fact, but I had to leave after that, so I never did find out who she was. Marty, what happened after I left? Were you able to get any information about her?"

Marty told them about how Carl had been able to identify her and how she'd seen the same woman in a newspaper article in a scrapbook Carl had shown her. "She was Dr. Ramsey's second wife, Lisbeth, and according to his administrative assistant, the love of his life."

"Whoa, Marty, back up. How did the administrative assistant become involved in this?" Jeff asked. "I thought you were talking about Carl."

She told them about her spur-of-the-moment decision to invite Sybil to lunch and the conversation she'd had with Sybil.

"That explains a lot," Laura said. "Poor thing. I feel sorry for her. It must have killed her each time he got married. I wonder what will happen to her now. Did she mention if she'd be working for Dr. Thurman?"

"No. I don't know why, but I got the sense he wasn't her favorite person. Maybe I'm reading a lot more into it than is there, but it was very clear her loyalty was to Dr. Ramsey. She mentioned a couple of things, kind of in passing, which I thought were odd."

"Marty, you know everything can be fodder when a murder case is involved, and you know how much I need to solve this one. Whatever she said could be relevant. What were the couple of things?"

"A yacht and a diary," Marty answered.

Jeff was quiet as he tried to figure out what they could mean, and then he said, "Tell me, as best you can, exactly what she said about both of those things."

Marty thought for a moment and then reiterated that part of her conversation with Sybil. "Jeff, I really doubt that a yacht or a diary has anything to do with Dr. Ramsey's murder. I probably shouldn't have said anything. The more I think about it, the more sure I am it means absolutely nothing."

Laura put her hand up, indicating she wanted to speak. "Guys, I know you trust my instincts, so I'm going to tell you what I'm feeling. As soon as Marty mentioned the diary, every psychic alarm bell I have in my body went off. Maybe I was a dog in a former life, because the hair on the nape of my neck stood on end, sort of like what happens to a dog when it's alarmed about something." She turned to Jeff and said, "If you don't do anything else tomorrow, talk to the doctor and find out what you can about that diary. The secret to the crime is there."

"Swell, Laura. Do I just walk up to him and say, 'Dr. Thurman, a friend of mine who's a psychic, said I need you to tell me about the diary you keep?' That should really get his attention," he said with a sense of frustration in his voice.

Duke had been lying underneath the table in his customary place, waiting for them to eat dinner and hoping that one of them would slip him a bite or two. He sensed the change in Jeff's manner, moved out from under the table, and put his head and one paw in Jeff's lap, silently acknowledging Jeff's frustration.

Jeff looked down at him and said, "Duke? This is a first. I think we're having a serious bonding moment." He gently petted the dog on his head and scratched his ears. "It's okay, Duke, honest, but I appreciate your concern for me."

Duke seemed to understand and returned to his place under the table.

"Okay, with that I think we need to take a break and have some dinner. Are you all ready?" John asked as he stood up and motioned for Max, his assistant, to do the same.

"We're always ready for your dinners, John. What's on the menu tonight?" Marty asked.

"Well, you know how I'm always looking for things I can make on the weekends and freeze. I saw a recipe recently for Swedish meatballs." He paused and looked at Les. "I see that grimace, Les, and I bet you're thinking of the way they used to be served years ago with grape jelly or ketchup on them. Trust me, these are a hundred percent better, and I'm serving them the way they were meant to be served, with a cream sauce over noodles. I know I'm going out on a limb here, but I can practically guarantee you're going to love them."

"Okay, I'm putty in your hands, John. I totally entrust my taste buds to you. What else is on the menu?" Les asked.

"Traditional Swedish side dishes of roasted baby red potatoes and carrots glazed with butter and fresh dill. Sound acceptable?"

"You had me at the roasted baby red potatoes. Sounds great. I mean it, John. Actually, I should give you a list of all the horrible foods my mother made me eat as a child. I know in your foodie hands you probably could make all of them desirable, not things I still have nightmares about," Les said laughing.

"Les, you never told me your mother made you eat horrible foods," Laura said.

"I kinda thought you'd be able to intuit it with your psychic abilities. No, I'm kidding. Let's just say not everyone had the Brady Bunch lifestyle growing up that you and Marty did. My mother worked two jobs after my dad split, and food was not a priority of hers. Also, she was one of the first flower children, and tofu was her main staple. Fried, baked, sautéed, scrambled, yuck! That's something I still have unpleasant dreams about, and yes, once she served me Swedish meatballs made with tofu."

"Well, in that case, it's probably a very good thing we have a resident chef here to cater to your porn food fantasies," Laura said.

"I never said I had porn food fantasies," Les protested.

"You didn't need to. I'm psychic, remember?"

"On that note, Max and I will leave to do our magic in the kitchen. We'll be back in a few minutes," John said

*****

"These are fabulous, John. I honestly didn't know you could make Swedish meatballs with something other than tofu. I apologize for my snarky look and what I was thinking a while ago, but given my history with tofu Swedish meatballs and grape jelly, I'm sure you can understand."

"No problem, Les. Since I'm seeing everyone nod in agreement, think I'll put this on the menu at the Red Pony, but maybe I should call them something else. You might not be the only one with bad memories of Swedish meatballs. I'm thinking maybe, Mama's meatballs. It gives it a homey feel. Anyway, I want to change the subject and get back to Jeff's investigation. Did I miss anything when I was in the kitchen? Jeff, have you decided what to do about the doctor and his diary?"

"I have no idea what to do. I'm sure something will come to me. Ironically enough, I have an interview with him tomorrow. He was tied up in surgery all day today, and I knew he'd be exhausted afterwards, so I told him to clear a little time for me in the afternoon.

I'll see what he says then. Maybe there's a logical explanation for it, like it's his calendar or something."

"It's not," Laura said. "Trust me on this one. Wish I knew more, but I don't."

"That's okay, Sis. You can't be expected to know everything," Marty said. "Jeff, I haven't had a chance to tell you that Dr. Ramsey's widow called me this afternoon and wants to talk to me about the appraisal of her husband's Shaker collection. I talked to Dick about what values I should use in the appraisal, and he hinted that he'd talked to Dr. Ramsey's attorney, and his widow may not be inheriting the estate."

"Do you know the name of his attorney?" Jeff asked.

"No, but it's probably on my computer. Dick was going to send me the lawyer's name and pertinent contact information, so I could send my report and bill to him when I'm finished."

"I'd like you to see if he's sent it when we go inside. I need to talk to the attorney and find out what I can from him. The doctor's widow might have found out that she wasn't going to inherit his estate when he died, although she seems to have enough money in her own right."

"Some people can never have enough money, and don't forget what Sybil said about hearing her yell at the doctor about her facelift. Anyway, I'm meeting her in the morning, and then in the afternoon I'm getting my hair done by the stylist who does the hair for one of the women who looks like the doctor's second wife. I'm thinking both of those women could be persons of interest."

"I agree, Marty, and I also think another person of interest could be Sybil. After all, she told you she was in love with the doctor and even told you she gave her life up for him. Maybe she just got fed up and realized he was never going to see her as anything other than as an administrative assistant."

"I know that's one scenario, Jeff, but I'd hate to think that about her. She really seemed completely shattered by his death. Don't forget she mentioned something about that husband who was upset about the way his wife's facelift turned out and said she didn't look like herself. Maybe he was angry enough to do something.

"What's his name, Marty? I'll give it to one of my men at the meeting tonight. He can check him out."

"Sybil didn't mention his name, but his wife's name is Missy Donaldson. You could probably get his name from Sybil."

"I'm sure I could, but I prefer that the less anyone knows, particularly when they might be a person of interest, the better it is. Everybody, I'm whipped, but I've got to go back to the station for that meeting. I'm still running on adrenalin, so I might as well work some of it off. I doubt if I could sleep. John, my compliments to the chef as always. Matter of fact, that's the first time I've ever had Swedish meatballs or Mama's meatballs, so I didn't have any bad memories I had to overcome," he said grinning at Les as he stood up.

"Right behind you Jeff. I'll walk Duke and see you in a few minutes," Marty said as she stood up from the table. Duke heard his name mentioned and walked over to Jeff. "I knew it. I just knew it was a matter of time until he forgot about me. Looks like you have a new best friend, Jeff," Marty said laughing.

Jeff looked down at the big black Lab who was wagging his tail and looking up at him. "Okay, Duke. I probably have enough gas in my tank to take you for a quick commune with nature before I have to head back to the station. Marty, would you see if Dick wrote you and if he did, I'd like the contact information for the attorney before I leave. I'll be there in a couple of minutes. Come on, Duke, let's go."

CHAPTER FOURTEEN

Marty carefully swung her legs over the edge of the bed the next morning as quietly as she could, but the movement caused Jeff to wake up anyway. "I'm sorry, Jeff. I know you didn't get in until late last night. I turned off the alarm, and I was trying so hard not to wake you."

"No problem, sweetheart. I need to get to work anyway. This case is going nowhere, and I think my future as the head of the Palm Springs detectives is about there as well."

"Jeff, it's way too early to be that pessimistic. I'm sure today will be a breakthrough day for you. Any luck having one of your people get information on Missy Donaldson's husband?"

"As a matter of fact, yes. His name is Paul Donaldson, and he's a dealer at the big Native American casino just off Interstate 10, south of Palm Springs. You've probably driven by it a hundred times. He works the noon to eight shift, and I'm hoping to get an appointment with his pit boss. I'm going to call him first thing this morning. I'll let you know what happens with that. You mentioned last night you have an appointment with Ashley Ramsey today. What time is it?"

"I have to be there at 10:00 this morning, and I have no idea what she wants to talk to me about. Now that my client is Dr. Ramsey's lawyer, and the appraisal is part of an estate of a deceased person, I have a confidentiality issue if she wants to know something like that."

"Yeah, I guess that could be dicey. Have you ever had to deal with that kind of a situation before?"

"Never, and truth be told, I'm dreading the meeting."

"Marty, just go with your instincts. You'll be fine. I mean, what's the worst thing she can do to you?"

"I could start with murder. After all, I think she is on your list of persons of interest, and I have no desire to become the victim of a person of interest."

"Point well taken. I'd tell you to take your gun with you, but that might be overkill at this point, pardon my pun."

She made a face at him. "Agreed, and I'd really feel uncomfortable with it in my purse. No, I'll just go to her house and see what she wants. I need to get on the computer and do a little research before I meet with her. There's bagels with all the fixings in the kitchen, and I'll put on a pot of coffee. Good luck, today," she said as she kissed him, put on her robe, and headed for the kitchen to make the coffee.

*****

Later that morning Marty pulled her car into the circular driveway in front of the Ramsey's low-slung Mid-Century Modern style house and parked. Palm Springs was a mecca for this type of architecture consisting of one story homes with a lot of glass, clean lines, and an outdoor-indoor feel. She hadn't really appreciated the architectural style when she'd conducted her appraisal at the Ramsey house, because she'd been so focused on the appraisal. Since a number of her appraisals had been in homes of that type, she'd become curious about it, and yesterday afternoon she'd spent some time researching the style.

Her research had indicated that many of the most noted architects of the mid-20th century had designed homes in the Coachella Valley.

She recalled that all of the homes she'd been in which were built in that style had consisted of wings in an L or U shape, usually with a pool in the center, and floor to ceiling windows which looked out at a pool, a desert landscape, or a golf course. With that type of flowing design, the homes were well-suited to entertaining, something the wealthy residents of Palm Springs were very good at.

She took a deep breath, opened her car door, walked up to the blue door, and rang the doorbell. A moment later, Lucille Jenkins, the Ramsey's housekeeper she had met during the home appraisal, opened the door and said, "It's good to see you again. Mrs. Ramsey is in the living room. May I get you some coffee?"

"No thanks, Lucille. I think I've had my quota for the day. You don't need to show me to the living room. I'm familiar with the house."

She walked down the hall to the large living room with exposed high wooden beams and glass walls that looked out at the pool and the desert hills beyond it. Ashley Ramsey was sitting in a large chair upholstered in a checkered pattern of cream, tan, and beige. Marty walked over to her, aware that Mrs. Ramsey was not going to stand up and greet her. She and Laura had once talked about a seminar Laura had taken on effective management. One of the things she'd told Marty was that the person who remained seated and waited for the other person to come to them became the dominant person in the relationship. Obviously, Mrs. Ramsey wanted to be the alpha dog in this relationship.

"Mrs. Ramsey, I'd like to express my condolences on the death of your husband. I know this must be a very difficult time for you, and if there's anything I can do to help you, I'd be happy to."

"Marty, I feel like I know you, so I hope you don't mind if I call you Marty," Ashley Ramsey said. "Thank you for coming on such short notice. I'd like to talk to you about the appraisal you were doing for my husband."

"Feel free to call me Marty. Actually, I'd like to ask you a question about your husband's antique collection. What caused him to collect Shaker items? It seems quite strange to see a collection like that out here in the California desert area."

Marty was telling the truth. She had been curious about the background of Dr. Ramsey's collection, but she also felt she needed a little time to ground herself before she had to tell Mrs. Ramsey that she couldn't discuss the monetary value of the collection, if that was why she'd asked Marty to come to her home.

"That's a fair question, and it's kind of an interesting story. His father grew up in Maine at a Shaker village. Since the Shakers were celibate, their children came to them through indenture or as foundlings. Keith's father was a foundling, but there was one little problem. When he was a young adult, he fell in love with a woman in a nearby village, and decided that he was not going to spend his life as a celibate. He and the woman left the village and came to California. Shortly after that Keith was born, their only child.

"Keith's father was very intelligent and realized that the farming he'd done while he'd lived at the Shaker village was not going to provide much of a life for his family, and that was all he knew how to do. He got a college degree and then he applied to medical school and was accepted. He scored high enough on his tests that he was given a full scholarship and several years later the family moved to Palm Springs. It was about the time that Palm Springs became the 'in place' for the very wealthy. He was one of the first plastic surgeons in the area, and he had no trouble establishing a thriving practice.

"I never met his father, but Keith told me his father had always felt guilty about turning his back on the Shaker community and their way of life. He decided that Keith needed to be aware of his father's heritage, at least what he knew about it, and so he started to collect Shaker items. From what Keith told me, when his father began to collect the items, they were quite inexpensive, almost throwaway items. It was only later that a market developed for them. Keith told me that his father used the term 'the items changed from outliving their utilitarian roots to items which were very desired by high-end collectors' to describe his collection. Fortunately, by that time, his father had the disposable income to become one of those high-end collectors."

"It's a stunning collection. I've never seen anything quite like it."

"From what Keith told me, it's rare enough that you probably never will. When his father died, Keith inherited the collection. His mother predeceased his father and Keith was an only child, so it all went to him. Obviously, he continued to add to the collection over the years. I think it was his way of paying homage to his father after he died, and Keith took over his lucrative medical practice."

"I've very much enjoyed having the chance to see the items in his collection. It felt like I was in my own private museum while I was doing the appraisal," Marty said.

"Well, I certainly hope that whoever I sell the collection to has the same feeling. Personally, the collection never did that much for me. I think it's pretty cold, you know, kind of sterile. So, the reason I asked you here this morning is to find out what the collection is worth. Since I'll be inheriting Keith's estate, I need to start making some preparations." She looked expectantly at Marty who felt sick to her stomach.

"Mrs. Ramsey, I haven't set a value on the collection yet. I need to do quite a bit of research, because the items are so rare and valuable."

"When do you think you'll have a value for it?" she asked.

"I hope to have it finished within two weeks, but there is a little problem."

"What's that?" Mrs. Reynolds asked.

"I've been informed that the appraisal is now the property of the estate." Marty took a deep breath and continued, "Since it is the property of the estate, Dr. Ramsey's attorney has instructed me to turn over the appraisal to him when I'm finished. Ethically, since the estate is my client, I can't discuss the value of the appraisal with anyone else."

"Are you insinuating that I should not be told what my husband's collection is worth? Is that what I'm understanding you to say?"

"Yes, Mrs. Ramsey, I'm afraid it is."

She was quiet for a moment, and Marty saw the mounting fury in her eyes and the telling tic of the throbbing muscle in her temple as she struggled to contain her anger. "Look, Marty, you must have some idea what it's worth. You can tell me that, since it won't be the exact figure that's used on the appraisal report, so that's not unethical. As a matter of fact, I could make it worth your trouble. How does $5,000 sound to you? No one needs to ever know about it."

"It sounds wonderful, Mrs. Reynolds," Marty said in all honesty as she stood up and slung her purse over her shoulder, "but I'd know about it, and I wouldn't be able to look at myself in the mirror. It was nice talking to you."

As she left the room she heard Mrs. Reynolds yell, "Okay, you drive a hard bargain. I'll give you $25,000." Marty walked down the hall and let herself out the door. When she got in her car, she took a deep breath, knowing she had not only just made a powerful enemy, but that the enemy could also be a murderer.

CHAPTER FIFTEEN

Marty's hands were shaking as she pulled out of the circular driveway after her meeting with Mrs. Ramsey. She looked at the clock on the dashboard and realized she had quite a bit of time before her appointment at the salon with Brett. She was trying to figure out where she should have lunch when she remembered that John had told her where the Red Pony food truck would be at lunchtime, and if she had a little time, to stop by and see him while she was in Palm Springs. She drove to the street he'd mentioned and easily saw it.

She stood in the long line of people who were ordering food at the Red Pony for quite a while, checking the messages on her phone as she waited. When her turn came, John looked out at her and said, "Marty, I don't think you've ever eaten at the Pony. Glad I told you where I'd be today when we were both leaving this morning. What can I get for you?"

"Surprise me, John. Whatever you serve me, I'm sure it will make my stomach happy."

"You're putting a lot of pressure on me. Let's see. Okay, I've got it. How does lasagna with some garlic bread sound? I made a couple of pans of it. It's almost gone, but there's enough left for you. Sound okay?"

"Sounds better than okay. No wonder there's such a long line waiting to eat here." She turned around and saw that the line behind her was as long as the one in front of her had been when she arrived. A few moments later John handed her a large paper plate with a steaming serving of lasagna with garlic bread.

"Looks delicious. Thanks." She handed him a five dollar bill and said, "Put the change in the tip jar, and thanks."

"Thank you. I hate to take your money, but there might be a riot on my hands if someone saw that I didn't take money from you, but I was taking money from everyone else."

"Thanks again, John. See you tonight." Marty took her food over to one of the portable picnic tables John had set out in front of the Pony. She spent the next few minutes thoroughly enjoying her lunch and congratulating herself for having thought to eat lunch at the popular food truck. Since she still had some time on her hands before her hair appointment, she decided to call Sybil and see how she was doing.

"You've reached the offices of Dr. Ramsey and Dr. Thurston. May I help you?" the voice that answered the phone asked.

"Yes, I'd like to speak with Sybil. Please tell her Marty Morgan-Combs is on the line."

The voice put her on hold, and a few moments later she heard Sybil's voice. "Marty, how nice of you to call. I assume you're not asking me to Armando's for lunch, since it's a little after the lunch hour."

"That's very true, and I'm glad to hear what sounds like a little smile in your voice today. I was just calling to see how you're doing. I've been thinking about you."

"Much better, thank you for caring. The initial shock is over, and now I'm trying to juggle patients, appointments, and surgeries. I wish I could tell you that everyone was gracious about things being cancelled, but that wouldn't be true. It seems that a lot of people thought that having a facelift or some other type of procedure would change their life, and they don't want to put that change on hold. I can't tell you how many people have asked for Dr. Thurston to do their surgery."

"I've heard that most plastic surgeons kind of do a little psychological counseling, if you will, regarding the fact that plastic surgery won't change their lives. I think I remember reading something about that in a magazine."

"I'm sure you did," Sybil said. "Dr. Ramsey always spent time with each patient trying to determine the reason they wanted the surgery. He was very ethical, and I know of two cases where he told the women he would not operate on them because he felt they wanted the surgery for the wrong reason."

"Wow, that is ethical. I'm impressed. How is Dr. Thurston standing up to the increased workload?"

"He's doing well. Actually, I think he's happy to have the extra business. Dr. Ramsey was always more in demand than he was. I always wondered if Dr. Thurston was a little jealous of him. I do have some good news. Dr. Thurston talked to me this morning and asked what my plans were for the future. I told him I hadn't made any decisions yet. He asked me if I would consider being his administrative assistant, since he would be taking over so many of Dr. Ramsey's patients."

"I thought you were the administrative assistant for the office, and that would include Dr. Thurston. Am I wrong?"

"Not really. I was, I guess I still am, the main administrative assistant for the office, but it was very clear that I was first and foremost Dr. Ramsey's employee. When I had free time, I helped Dr. Thurston, but usually other staff members did whatever he wanted."

"Do you think you could work with him?"

"I think so, even though they each had their own lifestyles. I believe I told you that Dr. Ramsey had been married several times. Dr. Thurston is a confirmed bachelor. His boat is his wife, and if he gets a larger one with all of the extra business he's going to have, I imagine that will be his priority. Can you hold, Marty? Denise just handed me a note that a caller says it's urgent that she speak with me."

"Of course, take your time."

The line was quiet for several moments and then Sybil came back on the line. "You are not going to believe this. That was Dr. Ramsey's wife. She told me she's hired a moving van to come to the office and remove Dr. Ramsey's Shaker collection. I told her Dr. Ramsey's attorney had called me this morning and told me that nothing was to be removed from the office. Actually, your husband said pretty much the same thing when I talked to him earlier today. He told me if I had any problems to give him a call. I don't think she'll send the moving van over this very minute, but I think I'll call your husband and tell him what she said."

"You absolutely should do that. Jeff can advise you on how to handle it. I don't know what's done in a case like that, but it shouldn't be your responsibility. I'll say goodbye for now, and I'll talk to you in a few days. You have my number. Please call me if I can help in any way. One last thing. Could you give me Lisbeth Ramsey's address?"

"Sure, here it is. Thanks for calling, Marty. I'll give your husband a call right now. Mrs. Ramsey sounded mad enough that she just might do something immediately. Good-bye."

Dr. Ramsey may have married her for her money, but I wouldn't be surprised if it was a decision he regretted, if my meeting with her and Sybil's phone call are indications of how much she cared for him.

Marty threw her napkin and paper plate in the trash barrel next to the Pony, waved to John, and walked over to her car, curious as to what the salon experience would be like.

CHAPTER SIXTEEN

When Marty pulled into the parking lot behind Brett Joseph's salon, she experienced a moment of panic. Almost every parking space in the lot was occupied, and a number of them contained limousines with uniformed drivers waiting for their rich employers. Most of the other spaces contained Bentleys, Mercedes Benzes, BMW's, and Ferraris. As she pulled into one of the few available empty spaces, she decided she'd been very smart to put all of her credit cards in her purse, convinced her initial thought that this appointment was going to be pricey was right.

She walked up the canopy-lined brick path that led to the salon and opened the door which had a stained glass inset of a woman's profile with her long hair flowing in the wind. A stunningly beautiful redhead sat behind what looked to Marty to be an authentic 18th century French Louis XV kidney shaped ladies writing table with a telephone and computer on it.

Marty looked around the salon and could hardly believe what she was seeing. The décor was in the mid-18th century French style, but to Marty's trained eye, she realized that everything she was looking at was authentic, from the furniture to the carefully chosen decorative items. About the only things that were contemporary were the items necessary to do business in a very high-end salon.

"May I help you?" the beautiful redhead asked in a voice thick with a French accent.

"Yes. My name is Marty Morgan-Combs, and I have an appointment with Brett Joseph."

The woman spent a moment looking at her computer, smiled up at Marty, stood up and said, "Please, follow me." She walked across the large room where there were a number of stations, all with beautiful and handsome men and women seated in chairs, as more beautiful women and handsome men did their magic on their clients.

"The changing room is over there. I'll introduce you to Brett's assistant, Claudia, and when you've changed, she'll shampoo your hair." She stopped at a basin outside of a room with a beveled glass door. A lovely young woman looked up and smiled at Marty.

"*Bon jour*, you must be Marty. I am Claudia. Please change into a gown, and I'll prepare you for *Monsieur* Joseph. His salon is through that door."

Never in my life have I been in a beauty salon where someone who was the owner or who worked in the salon had their own private room. This is simply unbelievable. I wonder if this is how it's done in France.

A few minutes later, after she'd put on her designer smock, thinking this was another first, she walked over to where Claudia was waiting for her. A woman stepped in front of Marty and put a number of what looked like dollar bills in Claudia's pocket. Claudia smiled at the woman and thanked her.

Swell. It never occurred to me that I'd have to tip someone who washed my hair. I hope I have some cash in my wallet, and I hope even more those were dollar bills and not five, ten, or twenty dollar bills the woman gave her. I am so out of my comfort zone here. I just hope it doesn't show.

As Claudia was getting Marty settled in the chair, another beautiful young woman walked over to Marty with a glass of champagne. "*Madame, Monsieur* Joseph always likes his clients to be relaxed. He has this champagne flown in from France. I hope you enjoy it." She placed the glass on the table next to Marty.

A glass of French champagne in the early afternoon at the toniest salon in the Palm Springs area. I'll bet my poor Midwest parents are spinning in their graves. Oh well, when in Rome...

She took a sip of the champagne and said, "Claudia, that really is delicious, but why does Mr. Joseph have it flown in from France? Couldn't he just buy a very good champagne here?"

"*Non*," she said. "Here in the United States it is called sparkling wine, and in Italy it is called Prosecco, but the word 'champagne' can only be used if the grapes are grown in the Champagne region of France, and it's made there. Being French, *Monsieur* believes it is far superior."

"Thank you. I learned something today."

"I am finished," Claudia said, as she wrapped the fluffiest towel Marty had ever seen around her head. Claudia walked over to the glass door just as it was opened and a stunning blonde woman walked out, closing the door behind her. A ray of sunlight glinted on the enormous diamond she wore on her finger, nearly blinding Marty.

"*Madame*," Claudia exclaimed, "you look beautiful! The haircut is perfect for you."

"Thank you," the woman said in a simpering voice. "Brett is such a genius. I can't imagine ever going to anyone else. See you in six weeks." She put a number of bills in Claudia's pocket, who smiled broadly at the woman and thanked her.

She turned back to Marty and said, "You can stand up now. I'll take you into *Monsieur's* room."

Claudia knocked on the door and a moment later a deep voice said, "Come in."

Claudia motioned for Marty to follow her, and they walked into the room. A very handsome man in his mid-50's with a silver pony tail and a large emerald earring in his left ear smiled at Marty and said, "*Bon jour.* You must be Marty. I am Brett. Please have a seat. Thank you, Claudia, that will be all."

"*Oui, Monsieur,*" she said as she closed the door behind her.

"What would you like me to do for you today?" Brett asked.

"I saw a woman at a restaurant and found out she's one of your clients. I loved her hair style. I don't know her last name, but her first name is Brandy. I could use a new look, and I'd like to try that type of hairstyle, if you think it would work on me."

"Ah yes, Brandy. She has been my client for many years," he said as he walked around the chair Marty was seated in, obviously assessing whether or not Brandy's hairstyle would work for her. "As a matter of fact, she was in here this morning for her monthly trim."

"A friend and I were having lunch at a restaurant and my friend knows her. Evidently she recently had a facelift, and she'd told my friend she wasn't very happy with the results."

"Normally I would never talk about a client of mine, but in this case, it has such a happy outcome I don't feel I'm divulging a confidence. Brandy was so excited, she was telling everyone here at the salon how thrilled she is with the way she looks."

"I'm happy for her, but that certainly is a one-eighty from what she told my friend," Marty said.

"That was how she felt right after she had the surgery," Brett said as he put his hands on Marty's head and moved his fingers back and forth through her hair, "and I must say she did look different. There really wasn't much of a resemblance between the pre-surgery Brandy and the post-surgery Brandy."

"What happened to change her mind?" Marty asked innocently.

"When she was here this morning she was telling everyone that her ex-husband wants a reconciliation. He dropped by her house last week to give Brandy her monthly alimony check, and a few days later he called her and said he'd forgotten how beautiful she is, and asked if she would consider a reconciliation. She couldn't believe it, but that's just half the story.

"Brandy said she'd been afraid to meet a man she'd been seeing for a while, because she wasn't sure what he would think about her facelift. She was going to meet him at Tommy Bahamas, but he surprised her by unexpectedly picking her up in his limousine an hour before they were to meet. He had his driver take them to Melvyn's. Everybody in Palm Springs knows that's the place for special moments, and it was for him. He took a little box out of his pocket and asked her to marry him. She said the diamond he gave her had to be at least six carats. She said it was the biggest diamond she'd ever seen, and trust me, Brandy knows diamonds. Brandy decided he was worth a lot more money than her ex, so she said yes. She's really excited by everything that's happened recently. Brandy said she wasn't very happy with the way she looked right after the surgery, but given her new ring, she's thinks it worked out very well."

"Wow. What a story. No wonder she's excited. Did she go to a local plastic surgeon? Maybe I should think about having some work done."

"Yes, but unfortunately the surgeon who did her facelift, Dr. Ramsey, was recently murdered. It's really a tragedy, because most of my clients have gone to him. Anyway, the doctor had a reputation for doing very good work, although I have wondered why so many of his patients bore a slight resemblance to each other, but as long as the women were happy with how they looked, who was I to say anything?" he said as he shrugged his shoulders in the classic French manner.

"Well, Brett, do you think I would look good with Brandy's hairstyle?"

"*Oui*, you would look amazing. First I will cut your hair, then I will blow dry it, and lastly, I will apply the highlights. You will look ten years younger when you leave, and what woman wouldn't like that?"

"I certainly would. Do you need me to do anything?"

"No, *cherié*, not a thing," he said as he reached for his scissors. "Just look straight ahead and be prepared to look absolutely stunning."

Two hours later, she stood in front of the receptionist who handed Marty a bill for Brett's services. She'd slipped ten one dollar bills into Claudia's pocket and had no idea if that amount was even near what she usually received, but that was all the cash she had. She steeled herself to look at the bill, took a deep breath, and thought she could have probably paid for a facelift with what her new hairdo had cost. She just hoped Jeff liked it.

Think I'll plead the fifth amendment on how much it cost, if he asks me. I don't think any man in the world would feel a new hairstyle was worth that amount. I think in some parts of the United States, people could make a down payment on a house with the amount of money I just spent.

CHAPTER SEVENTEEN

When she got in her car, she decided she had enough time to drive to Lisbeth Ramsey's home and see if she had any thoughts about the murder of her ex-husband. She hoped the children weren't home, because even though Lisbeth had left Dr. Ramsey for another man, the children were Dr. Ramsey's children, and they were bound to be upset by his death.

All the way there she kept looking at herself in the rear-view mirror and finally acknowledged that as expensive as her hairdo had been, she really did look ten years younger. She knew she wasn't the beauty that Lisbeth Ramsey was touted to be, but she felt she'd pass Lisbeth's inspection.

Marty pulled in the driveway of a well-kept Mediterranean style desert home in an upper-class neighborhood. While it wasn't as large or as architecturally interesting as Dr. Ramsey's home, it was certainly much nicer than the average home in Palm Springs or anywhere else, for that matter.

She rang the doorbell, and a moment later a woman's voice asked, "Who is it?"

"My name is Marty Morgan-Combs. I'm here in a totally unofficial capacity. My husband is the lead detective on the case involving your ex-husband's murder, and I'm trying to help him. I wonder if you could spare a couple of minutes to talk to me. I'm putting my driver's license in front of the peep-hole on the door, so you can see my identification. I really would like to talk to you."

The door opened and one of the most beautiful women Marty had ever seen said, "Please come in. I rather doubt that I know anything that can help you, but I'm willing to try. My children are devastated by the death of their father, and quite frankly, so am I."

When Marty looked at Lisbeth closely she noticed her red-rimmed eyes and the dark circles under her eyes. She said, "I'm sure this is a very difficult time for all of you. I understand Dr. Ramsey was a very well-respected and loved doctor. I just wonder if there's anything you might know, however inconsequential you may think it is, that could help my husband solve the case He's so busy following leads and speaking to persons of interest, that I thought I might be able to find out something for him."

"Let's go into the living room to talk. Fortunately, the children went to a friend's house after school today. I'm sure some people think I should keep them out of school for a while, but his death is enough of a shock. I want to keep up some semblance of a normal routine for them. My friend insisted they come over and play with her children, plus the family has three dogs and since I'm highly allergic to dogs, I can't allow my children to have one."

Marty found it hard to believe that someone as beautiful as Lisbeth Ramsey was also one of the most gracious women she'd ever met, but she seemed to be. "Mrs. Ramsey, I really don't know where to begin. I guess I'll just start with the big question. Can you think of anyone who would want harm to come to your husband?"

Lisbeth was quiet for several moments while she considered Marty's question, and then she said, "Believe me, I've asked myself that question a million times since I got the phone call that Keith had been murdered, and the answer is a resounding no. If you've talked to people, and I'm sure you have, you're probably aware that I left Keith for the man who cleaned our swimming pool. I can't say I'm very proud of it, but I did. It was for a reason as old as time – Keith was spending a lot more time and energy on his medical practice than he was on me or the children. I felt like a single mom, and then since

I felt I was single, I decided to have a fling. Unfortunately, or fortunately, it didn't work out, and it wound up being the stupidest thing I've ever done."

"We all make mistakes," Marty said. "but it sounds like yours had a few consequences."

"You might call them bitter consequences," Lisbeth said. "Keith married Ashley on the rebound. He really didn't need her money, but she, in my opinion, took advantage of a very vulnerable, hurting man, and, along with her money, was able to get him to marry her. It was about that time that I realized the horrible mistake I had made."

"Did Keith ever know you regretted your decision?"

"Yes. I knew he had remarried, but I called him one day and asked him to come over to the house. I told him it was about our daughter, Dani. Dani had Keith wrapped around her little finger, and there was nothing he wouldn't do for her. Really, it was quite easy."

"So, he came over here and then what?"

"After we talked about Dani, I told him there was something I needed to say. I told him I loved him, and that I'd never stopped loving him. I told him I had made a horrible mistake as well as the reasons I'd done it. I asked for his forgiveness."

"Did he give it to you?"

"He gave me more than that. He told me he still loved me, and that his marriage to Ashley was a disaster, to use his words. He said he'd like to see me and maybe there would be a chance we could reconcile. I reminded him that he would have to get a divorce if we did."

"What did he say?" Marty asked.

"He said a divorce was already on his mind. It may sound tawdry, but from that time, which was about six months ago, we met here, or at hotels, or restaurants. We talked and laughed, and both of us realized we wanted to be together permanently. We wanted to be a family again."

"Did he ask Ashley for a divorce?"

"That I'll never know. He was planning on asking her the evening before he was murdered. I didn't talk to him the next day, because he had a full surgery schedule, and it was my turn to help in the children's classrooms. I help a half-day a week in each of their classes." She put her head in her hands and started sobbing. After a moment, she looked up at Marty and tearily said, "If I hadn't left him, he'd still be alive. Ever since I heard about his murder, I've blamed myself for it every minute I've been awake."

Marty saw a box of Kleenex on the table, pulled one from the box, and took it over to where Lisbeth was sitting. "Here, take this. Lisbeth, I wish there was something I could say to ease your pain, but I don't know what it would be. This truly is a tragedy, not only for him, but for you and the children. Let me ask you this. Do you think Ashley could have been the murderer?"

"Quite honestly, I have no idea. Certainly, I've considered it. One scenario I have is that he told Ashley about us and that he wanted a divorce. She thought about it all the next day and then went to his office and murdered him, but that's strictly a thought. I have nothing solid to back it up with."

"Let's consider another possibility. Could it have something to do with his medical practice?" Marty asked. "There are rumors that several of the women he performed facelifts on bear a resemblance to you. Did he ever mention that to you?"

"Really? He never said anything about it, and I don't understand what that would have to do with his murder, anyway."

"Lisbeth, you are a beautiful woman, and even if he tried to recreate you in another woman, maybe the woman or her husband preferred her to look like her old self, just better, but that's nothing more than conjecture on my part."

"If that's true, it's kind of weird."

"Lisbeth, what about his associate, Dr. Thurston? Do you know much about him?"

"No, I don't. It was strictly a business arrangement. I don't think he and Keith ever saw each other outside of the office. At least when I was married to him, he didn't. Dr. Thurston doesn't seem like a very sociable man, although I have to say, I don't feel like I know him."

"I understand Dr. Ramsey was married prior to you. What about his first wife?"

"I never met her, but I understand it was a very amicable divorce. They were just two people who probably never should have gotten married in the first place. As far as I know, she went back to Atlanta. She and Keith met when they were both residents at Cedars Sinai Hospital in Los Angeles. She was also a plastic surgeon. From what he told me, there was no alimony involved, they just split up the furniture, and since they were both getting ready to start their medical practices, they really didn't have any money to speak of. She would have had absolutely no reason to wish him harm. I'm certain of that."

"What about his administrative assistant, Sybil? How well do you know her?"

"I feel like I know her very well. As a matter of fact, she's the godmother for my daughter, Dani. Keith thought the world of her. I often wondered if she thought of him as more than just her employer, but if she did, I don't think Keith was aware of it. And there was really no reason for me to think that, other than a woman's intuition. She was totally devoted to him and his practice." She looked at her watch and said as she stood up, "I'm sorry to end this, but I really need to pick up my children from my friend's house. I'm a few minutes late as it is, and they don't need any more trauma in their lives right now."

"Thank you very much for taking the time to talk to me. I wish there was something I could say that would help, but words seem so meaningless at a time like this. Here's my business card. If you think of anything, feel free to call me."

"I will," Lisbeth said as she closed the door behind Marty. Marty was standing just outside the front door looking at her phone to see if she had any messages when Lisbeth opened the garage door and backed out in a late model Ferrari.

Hmm, must have been a nice divorce settlement, Marty thought. *Don't think cars like that come cheap.*

CHAPTER EIGHTEEN

Jeff had called Sybil at Dr. Ramsey's office earlier that morning and asked if she could meet with him for a little while. Although he'd spoken with her briefly on the night of Dr. Ramsey's death, he wanted to do an in-depth interview with her. As Dr. Ramsey's administrative assistant, she probably knew more than anyone else in the office about Dr. Ramsey and Dr. Thurston.

She agreed to meet with him before his appointment with the pit boss at the casino where Paul Donaldson worked. The pit boss, Hugh Lawson, had told Jeff he'd switched his shift with one of the other pit bosses, so the man could attend his son's elementary school graduation, and he'd be happy to meet with Jeff during his lunch break.

When Jeff walked into the plastic surgery suite, he was again pleasantly surprised at how tastefully decorated it was. Although he'd been there the night of the murder, he hadn't paid all that much attention to it. He didn't know what he was expecting, but it certainly hadn't been anything as plush as the reception area he was in. He'd seen some of Marty's photographs of Dr. Ramsey's Shaker collection and the furniture had looked pretty uncomfortable to him, so the casual relaxed feeling of the room was better than he thought it would be.

An attractive woman about his age looked out at him from behind the reception counter and said, "May I help you?"

"Yes, I'm Detective Jeff Combs. I have an appointment with Sybil. By any chance would you be her?"

"That would be me," she said, "I'll buzz you in, and we can go into my office." She turned to a woman who was standing at a file cabinet and said, "Denise, would you take over for me? I shouldn't be that long." She pressed a button underneath the counter, and a moment later Jeff was following her down the hall to her office.

"Detective, please, have a seat," Sybil said as she gestured to a large upholstered chair. "Your wife was gracious enough to ask me to lunch yesterday, but I fear I wasn't very good company. I'm much better today, but I'm still having a hard time dealing with Dr. Ramsey's death. I mean, when you've worked for someone for over twenty years, and then they're gone in an instant, it kind of turns your world upside down."

If she's the murderer, she's missed her calling. She'd make a great actress, Jeff thought.

"This shouldn't take long, Sybil. As you know, Dr. Thurston was the one who discovered the body at approximately 6:30 in the evening. He told me he'd returned to the office to check his surgery schedule for the following day, since his home computer wasn't working and that he'd seen light on in Dr. Ramsey's office. I'd like to know what time you left the office and if you saw anything suspicious prior to that."

"Detective, if you're asking me for an alibi, I don't have one. I left the office at 5:30, just like I usually do. I went home, changed clothes, and took my two dogs, a Jack Russell terrier and a cocker spaniel, on a long walk. After our walk, I decided to have a glass of wine while I watched the news and thought about what I'd fix for dinner. About 7:30 I'd just starting making my dinner when, as you know, I received the call from you that Dr. Ramsey had been murdered. That's all I can tell you."

"Sybil, I hate to ask this, but did you talk to anyone or see anyone while you were walking your dogs?"

"Detective, you might as well ask me outright if anyone can corroborate my story, and the answer is no. As a matter of fact, I remember thinking how odd it was that no one else was walking their dog that evening. Usually I run into a couple of other people at that time of night, but unfortunately I didn't see anyone."

"Did you receive any calls or talk on the phone to anyone during that time?"

"Again, Detective, the answer is no. Believe me, I wish I had an alibi for that time frame, but I don't. What I can tell you is that I was probably the most loyal employee Dr. Ramsey ever had. I've known his last two wives, and I'm even the godmother to Dani, his daughter by his second wife. Quite simply, I've devoted the last twenty years of my life to him and his practice. I've never married, and I have a very limited social life. My priority has been Dr. Ramsey. Do you have any other questions?"

"Have you noticed anything unusual either recently or in the last few years regarding Dr. Ramsey or Dr. Thurston? I'll consider whatever you tell me to be confidential. I'm just trying to figure out who the murderer is, and quite frankly, I don't have much to go on."

She looked out the window for several minutes, her hand cupping her chin, and then she turned to him. "Detective, I'm going to tell you a couple of things, but quite honestly, I don't see how they could have anything to do with Dr. Ramsey's murder."

"Sybil, please tell me whatever you know, no matter how inconsequential you may think it is. It's been my experience that often the most trivial thing is the one that helps to solve a crime."

She walked over to the door and made sure it was securely closed, then she turned around and said, "I've been asked by Dr. Thurston to remain here and become his administrative assistant, and I've agreed to do so. It makes sense in a number of ways. I know the patients and the office procedures, plus it guarantees me a job, although I don't think I'd have a problem getting another job."

"I'm sure you're right. I would think that with the number of plastic surgeons in the Palm Springs area, someone who has been an administrative assistant to one for that many years would be very employable."

"That's true, but I really don't want to go through that." She looked at her watch and said, "I do have a number of people I need to call, but there are a couple of things that cause me concern."

"Anything you can tell me would be appreciated."

"Well, the first thing is that one time I heard an argument between Dr. Ramsey and Dr. Thurman. It was after the office was closed, and I was just getting ready to leave. I'm sure they thought I'd already left. Anyway, Dr. Thurman was accusing Dr. Ramsey of making too many of his facelift patients look alike. He even hinted that Dr. Ramsey was trying to recreate his former wife, Lisbeth, when he did facelifts on his patients."

"What's your feeling on that?" Jeff asked.

"Quite honestly, I know that Lisbeth was the love of his life. He was heartbroken when she left him, and leaving him for the pool man didn't help his self-esteem. I do have to say that some of the patients he's performed surgery on tend to look like her, but I always thought it was because she was so beautiful he was just trying to recreate her beauty. I never saw it as a liability, but a couple of the patients weren't too happy with their results."

She told him how Brandy had called several times, and Missy's husband had called and complained to Dr. Ramsey about how they looked following their facelift surgeries. Sybil told him that neither one had called in the last few days.

"Do you know if Dr. Ramsey was ever sued by a patient for malpractice or if any other patients were unhappy?" Jeff asked.

"No, as a matter of fact I heard him say many times that he was probably one of the few plastic surgeons in the Palm Springs area who hadn't been sued for malpractice. He thought of it as quite a testament to his surgical abilities."

"Sybil, back to the argument you overheard. How did Dr. Ramsey respond to Dr. Thurman?"

"He told Dr. Thurman that the women bearing a resemblance to one another probably occurred because he thought of his ex-wife as the most beautiful woman in the world, and while he was operating he probably had her in his mind. He said all of his patients had been happy with the results, so it really wasn't a problem."

"Was that before he operated on Brandy and Missy?"

"Yes, come to think of it, it was, but as I said, after their initial phone calls, we haven't heard from either of them recently. Dr. Ramsey was very charismatic and very persuasive. If there were other patients who questioned how they looked, I imagine he talked to them when they returned for their post-surgery exams, because I certainly never heard anything."

"Sybil, I know I've taken up quite a bit of your time and you have a lot to do, but is there anything else you can think of that I should know? You mentioned two things."

"Detective, this is probably nothing, but I just think it's odd."

"Sybil, as I said earlier, nothing is too small when I'm trying to solve a murder case. Please, tell me what it is."

"Okay. Several times I've seen Dr. Thurman writing things in a little black notebook, you know, kind of a diary thing. It's not done in a casual manner, like you'd write in an appointment book or something like that. Each time I've seen him, he's been furiously writing. As soon as I walked into his office, he looked uncomfortable and shoved the book in a drawer."

"Do you have any idea what he was writing down?"

"No, but there was something weird about it, because he was always so intense when he was doing it. It struck me as strange."

"I'd feel the same way if I saw someone doing that. Last question. Did Dr. Ramsey ever say anything to you about Dr. Thurston's writings?"

"No, and I'd be willing to bet he never saw him do it. You see, each of the doctors had separate offices and nurses. The only things they shared were the reception room, the billing clerk, the file room, and the surgical center. The reception area was like the suite's halfway point. Dr. Ramsey's offices are to the left, and Dr. Thurston's offices are to the right. That's why I thought it was odd that Dr. Thurston discovered Dr. Ramsey's body. Normally, they never went into each other's offices unless they came to me and asked if one or the other was free."

"What do you mean, free?"

"Just whether or not they had a patient or were in surgery. Their practices were separate, and although they called themselves partners, in reality Dr. Thurston paid Dr. Ramsey a monthly fee for the things they shared along with the utilities and insurance and his suite of offices. I know each of them carried their own malpractice insurance, and Dr. Thurston's employees were paid directly by him. I really must go, Detective. I hope some of what I've told you helps with your investigation."

Jeff stood up and put out his hand. "I'm not quite sure what any of it means yet, but at some point, it will all fit together. Here's my card, and please feel free to call me if you think of anything else. My cell phone number is on the card, so you can call me at that number 24/7. Thank you so much for your time."

CHAPTER NINETEEN

Jeff left the surgery office and headed west to the casino where Paul Donaldson worked. He had an appointment to meet with Hugh Lawson, Paul's pit boss, while he was on his lunch break. He parked in the large parking lot and seeing the number of cars in the lot, he once again realized what a boon the recent casino additions had been to the economy of the Palm Springs area.

Hugh had told him to take the elevator to the third floor, turn left, and at the end of the hall was the employees' lunchroom area where they could meet. He said to walk in, and he was the one with grey hair and a grey mustache. When Jeff entered the lunchroom he easily spotted Hugh and walked over to where he was sitting. Hugh had been watching for him and stood up, his lunch on the table in front of him.

"You must be Detective Combs. I'm Hugh Lawson. Please have a seat. May I get you some coffee?"

"No thanks, I think I've had enough for the day. I promise not to take up much of your tine. I just have a few questions I'd like to ask you."

"Fire away. You mentioned it was about the death of some plastic surgeon. I've never been to one, and to my knowledge, no one in my family has ever had any work done, but hey, this is Palm Springs. Be willing to bet that half the people in the casino downstairs have been to one."

"I'd agree. I'm more interested in an employee who works as a dealer in the casino, and I understand you're the pit boss for the section of the casino where he works. His name is Paul Donaldson."

"Yes, Paul works for me. He works the noon to 8:00 p.m. shift. Actually, he's one of the best-liked dealers here at the casino. His tables are always full."

"I don't quite know what you mean by 'his tables are always full.' Could you explain?" Jeff asked.

"Sure," Hugh said taking a long drink from his iced tea. "When a dealer's popular with the players, their tables usually have more players than the other tables. All you have to do is walk through a casino, and you can see for yourself which dealers are more popular."

"Let me interrupt before you go any further. Why would one dealer be more popular than another?"

"It's all about money. If you win at a certain table, you tend to go back to that table. And the more people at the table means more winners and more money changing hands."

"Does that translate into bigger salaries for certain card dealers? Pardon my ignorance, but I really don't know how casinos operate."

"That's a yes and no question, Detective. You see the base pay of all of the dealers is pretty much the same. There may be an adjustment for longevity or something like that, but basically, they're pretty much all paid the same. The operative word here is 'paid the same.' What makes the difference in how much money they make is the amount in tips they take home."

"So, they receive tips from the players at their table, is that what you're saying?"

"Yes. Consider that the average dealer is getting a base pay of around $25,000 a year, yet some of them take home upwards of $60,000. I've even known a couple of dealers who made it to the $100,000 level, but that's pretty unusual. When people win big at the tables, they often give the dealer a big tip. It seems like the later it is at night, or should I say, early morning, the bigger the tips. I imagine the amount of alcohol they've consumed by that time has something to do with it as well."

"Wow, I had no idea. I must be in the wrong profession. If Paul is so popular and the tips are bigger the later it is, why doesn't he work a later shift? I'd think he could make more money."

"I've talked to him about doing that, but he's a real family man. He has a wife, Missy, and two kids. He doesn't want to be away from them at night. Pretty commendable in today's world, if you ask me," Hugh said.

"I agree. What do you know about his wife?"

"He seems devoted to her. She had some plastic surgery done a couple of months or so ago, and at first Paul was furious about it. I guess his wife, Missy, was happy with it, but he said she didn't look like she had before the surgery. He finally decided that was probably the whole point of it, and he even told me a couple of days ago that she really does look terrific. He said he was glad he hadn't sued the doctor or done something stupid, but that he just hadn't been prepared for having his wife look as different as she does."

"What's his personality like? Would you say he's easy-going or would he be the type that might easily lose his temper?"

"Paul Donaldson is one of the most likeable, easy-going people I've ever met. To give you an idea of how easy-going he is, he recently took several days of vacation time, and he and Missy took ten girls from his daughter's Girl Scout group on a camping trip. I mean, what dad is going to do that unless he's been guilted or shamed into doing it? But Paul was really excited about it. That's the kind of guy he is and probably why he's such a popular dealer. If there was one man I'd rely on to do the right thing, it would be Paul Donaldson."

"Hugh, you've been more than helpful. I can't thank you enough for taking time during your lunch break to talk to me. I see you have a little bit of your sandwich left and a couple of cookies. Enjoy, and again, thanks for your time. I can find my way out."

Jeff stood up and held out his hand. The men shook hands, and as Jeff left the casino, he was convinced that he could scratch one person off of his list of persons of interest, Paul Donaldson.

CHAPTER TWENTY

When Jeff got in his car, he took his phone out and checked for messages. There was one from Sybil. He called her back, wondering if she'd remembered something.

He recognized her voice when she answered the phone. "Sybil, it's Detective Combs. I have a message on my phone asking me to call you. What can I do for you?"

"Detective, I received a call a little while ago from Dr. Ramsey's wife, Ashley. She sounded really angry and told me she'd arranged for a moving van to come to the doctor's office and remove his collection of antiques. I happened to be talking to your wife when she called, and she told me I should call you. I don't know what to do."

"Lock the front door right now, and I'll call Dr. Ramsey's attorney. I wanted to talk to him anyway. I'll call you back once I've spoken with him. Don't let Dr. Ramsey's wife or anyone from the moving company into the office. Do you have any patients who will be coming to the office today?"

"Yes. Dr. Thurston's surgery schedule is filled for the rest of the afternoon, and I believe you have an appointment with him late this afternoon. What should I do?"

"I recall seeing a back door when I was there earlier. Call the patients and tell them to enter the office through that door. You could say something like the police have suggested you make some changes at the office. If you can't get in touch with someone and they show up at the front door, verify who it is, and then let them in. I don't believe Mrs. Ramsey would have any way of knowing what patients would be having surgery today. I'll get back to you in a few minutes."

Jeff placed a call to Roseanne, his secretary, at the station. "Roseanne, I want you to go into my office and get the file on the murder of Dr. Ramsey. I think it's on the right side of my desk. I'll hold while you do it."

A moment later she came back on the phone. "Detective, I found the file. What do you want to know?"

"I need the name and telephone number of Dr. Ramsey's attorney. I believe I wrote it down on the inside of the file folder. Take a look and see if you can find it."

A moment later she was back on the line. "His name is Roger Sills. Here's his number." She gave it to him.

"As always, thanks. I should be in the office in about twenty minutes. See you then."

He called the lawyer's office, and a friendly female voice answered the phone. "This is attorney Roger Sills' office. How may I help you?"

"This is Detective Combs with the Palm Springs Police Department. May I speak with Mr. Sills? Tell him this is regarding the death of his client, Dr. Ramsey."

"Detective, he just walked into the office. Please hold."

"This is Roger Sills, Detective. What can I do for you?"

"I'd like to talk to you at length about your deceased client, Dr. Keith Ramsey, but I have an immediate problem regarding him. I've just received a call from his administrative assistant, Sybil, telling me that Dr. Ramsey's wife just called her and told her she was coming to the office with a moving van and was going to remove the antique collection Dr. Ramsey had in his office."

"She has no right to it. As a matter of fact, his entire estate is part of a trust which will be distributed equally to his ex-wife, Lisbeth, and their two children, not to her. Dr. Ramsey appointed me to act as the trustee of his trust in the event of his death, and I will be administering the distribution of the trust assets shortly. When did Sybil think she would be there?"

"From what she said, I gathered it was imminent."

"I just looked at my calendar, and I see that my appointment for this afternoon cancelled. I was going to spend the rest of the afternoon doing paperwork, but I think I better take care of this problem. I'm going to leave for Dr. Ramsey's office right now. Would you call Sybil and tell her I'm on my way? I've met her before, so that shouldn't be a problem."

"Of course. I told her to lock the door, call Dr. Thurston's patients, and tell them to enter through the back door. You might want to do the same."

"Will do, and thanks for the call. According to the terms of Dr. Ramsey's trust he disinherited his widow. Now I wonder what she's planning on doing with the antiques in the house. When I'm finished at Dr. Ramsey's office, I probably need to get a court restraining order prohibiting her from doing anything with the collection that's in the house. Actually, as I recall, title to the house is vested in the name of the trust, so I should be able to get an order for her to vacate the premises, which, under the circumstances, would probably be a good idea."

"I agree, but that's your area of expertise, not mine," Jeff said. "I'll be at my office the rest of the afternoon. When you get the situation under control and if you have a minute, I'd appreciate it if you could call me and let me know what happened. Here's my number."

"Will do. Talk to you later."

CHAPTER TWENTY-ONE

When Marty drove into the driveway of the compound and parked her car, she saw that Jeff wasn't there yet, but it looked like everyone else was. She glanced over at the gate where her faithful companion, Duke, was waiting for her just inside the gate. She opened it and bent down to pet him.

"I'm home, big guy. How about we go for a walk before I show the new me to everyone. Let's go." She and Duke walked around to the far side of the compound houses where he spent a few minutes communing with nature. They walked back to the gate, but instead of Duke following her into the house as he usually did, he laid down again, watching the street in front of the compound and the driveway. "Come on, Duke. Time to go into the house like we always do when I get home."

After five minutes of cajoling and pleading, it became apparent to Marty that Duke had some other agenda in mind, and that agenda was waiting for Jeff to come home. Clearly, Jeff had displaced Marty on Duke's list of people he was most loyal to. She glanced at the courtyard, aware that none of the residents were there for the pre-dinner sharing of the news of the day. As she walked into her house she felt a pang of jealousy, which wasn't an emotion she'd felt since her husband, Scott, had told her he was leaving her for his secretary.

To think I trained Duke and spent all that time putting pink booties on him, and then Jeff completely takes him away from me. I can't believe it. It would serve both of them right if I got a new puppy, one that was entirely mine.

The second thought she had was that she was glad Duke and Jeff had bonded, because the first few days after they returned from their honeymoon had been touch and go as to whether or not Duke was going to accept the big, handsome detective who had clearly won the heart of his mistress. It had been hard enough for Duke to accept that Jeff was going to be living in his and Marty's house, but to add insult to injury, the man was now sleeping in the bed right beside Marty, a place Duke had occupied from the time he'd been a puppy.

Marty finally decided that nothing would be gained by being jealous and decided to compliment Jeff on his ability to win Duke over. Even so, she could hear a little voice in the back of her head saying, "A new puppy really wouldn't be all that big a deal, and Duke would even have someone to play with."

Well, that's one thing I don't need to make a decision about this minute. Plenty of time for that later on.

She changed into jeans and a pale pink blouse which accentuated her new hairdo and the highlights Brett had spent so much time applying. She looked at herself in the mirror and knew Jeff was going to be happy with the results. She decided to refresh her makeup, so the version of the new Marty would be complete.

A few minutes later she walked out into the courtyard, noticing the twinkling lights which had been strung on the big tree in the center of the courtyard, which were always a welcoming sight to the residents. "Wow, you look fantastic. What's the occasion?" Max asked, looking up from where he was putting wine glasses and wine on the table.

"No special occasion. I wanted to have my hair done by a man who is the stylist for a woman who was a person of interest in the Dr. Ramsey case. Although I think she can be crossed off the list as a person of interest, I did get a bonus with this new do. I just hope Jeff likes it," she said.

"Jeff loves it," a booming voice said from the gate. "Come here and let me see it," the big detective said, Duke at his heels. "Marty, you look fantastic. Turn around." She twirled and he caught her up in his arms. "No matter what happens in the Dr. Ramsey case, with you for a wife, I have to be the luckiest man in the world. You were beautiful when I met you, when I married you, and when we honeymooned," he grinned suggestively, "but, this is a step beyond. I better be careful, or you'll be leaving me for one of those Palm Springs sugar daddies we always hear about."

Marty kissed him and whispered, "Jeff, trust me. You don't have a thing to worry about, other than the fact that we may be having an addition to the family."

"Whoa, lady, we talked about that, and you assured me that was not possible. I'm a little long in the tooth for the daddy gig, and sweetheart, I hate to say it, but I think you are, too." He pushed her away and looked at her. "Tell me you're not going to say what I'm thinking."

She laughed and looked down at Duke. "I'm thinking maybe I need to get a puppy, because it's becoming very clear to me that you've stolen my dog's affection."

"Marty, are you serious? Do you have any idea what I'm thinking?"

"Yes, and the answer is no. The only little addition to our family may be a puppy. I'm in the thinking stage about it."

"Well, when you get ready to take it beyond the thinking stage, I think I should be the first to know. By the way, you really do look gorgeous. Do I want to know what it costs to look that gorgeous?"

"No. Very simply, no. We could probably buy a kennel and all the inhabitants in it for what I paid for this new do, but if you're happy with the way I look, then it was worth every penny."

"Tell you what, Marty. Consider it my treat."

"Easy for you to say, since you don't have a clue how much it cost."

"Okay, that's enough, you two lovebirds," Laura said. "Marty, you look great. Love the new do, and you look ten years younger. Think I need the name of this wizard you went to."

"I'm happy to give you his name, but I'd advise you to sell all your stocks and bonds before you go. You might also think about refinancing the houses here in the compound as well," Marty said laughing as the three of them walked over to the large table where Max was finishing up setting the table for dinner. A few minutes later they were joined by Les and John, who also told Marty how terrific she looked.

"Okay, everyone, thanks. Now, enough about me. By the way, I had lunch at The Red Pony today, and I can confidently tell you that our fellow resident, John, outdid himself. Plus, I had to wait in line for fifteen minutes before I could even place my order."

"I'm not surprised, considering the meals we're lucky enough to have here, compliments of Chef John. I think we're the luckiest guinea pigs in the world," Les said as he smiled at John. "I really mean it. Whenever I have to go to some dinner after a gallery opening or whatever, I always wish I was at home eating your food instead."

"Thank you, one and all," John said. "A little later I'll be serving chimichangas, hopefully the way Laura likes them. I've made a fruit salad to go with them, and for dessert we'll be having a Mexican chocolate custard, but first I'm interested in hearing about what's happening with the Dr. Ramsey case. Actually, I think all of us are. I have to make a quick trip to the kitchen, but just for a minute, so don't start without me."

CHAPTER TWENTY-TWO

"Okay, I'm back," John said. "Now you can start. Jeff, since you're the lead detective on the case, what happened today?"

Jeff told them about his meetings with Sybil and Hugh. He sighed and said, "After talking to Sybil, either she's a very, very good actress, or she's completely innocent. I'd prefer to think she's innocent, because I liked her, although it wouldn't be the first time I've liked someone who later turned out to be a murderer."

"Did she have an alibi?" Marty asked. "When I had lunch with her, that never came up, and I've been wondering about it. I guess what I'm thinking is if she is the murderer, I would assume she'd have an alibi, or at least the semblance of one."

"No, she has absolutely no way of verifying that she took her dogs out for a walk when she got home, watched the news on television, and was fixing her dinner when she got the phone call about Dr. Ramsey's murder. I agree with you Marty, usually the first thing a murderer will do is establish an alibi, one that's as air-tight as possible. The fact that she has none certainly indicates a sense of innocence, but then again, you have to wonder if that was the whole reason for not having an alibi, to make it seem she was too innocent to have one," Jeff said.

"That's an angle I never thought of."

"After years of investigating crimes, I've learned that you look at everything. You turn all the facts upside down, inside out, and then examine them on their face value. So, the answer to your question is no, she doesn't have an alibi."

"Jeff, right after I finished lunch at the Pony I called her to see how she was doing," Marty said. "We talked for a while, and then she had another call. It was from Dr. Ramsey's wife. She told Sybil she'd hired a moving van, and they were on their way to the office to pack up his antique collection. I told her to call you, did she?"

"Yes, I'd just gotten out of a meeting with Paul Donaldson's boss, when I saw that she'd called. By the way, from what his boss told me, Paul's someone I think we can cross off the suspect list. His boss said although Paul wasn't thrilled with how his wife looked immediately after her surgery, he's gotten to really like the way she looks now. According to his boss, the guy is a combination of a saint and an Eagle Scout.

"Anyway, I returned Sybil's call, and long story short, I called Roger Sills, Dr. Ramsey's attorney, and he went over to the office to take care of the problem. He told me that, according to Dr. Ramsey's trust, everything goes to his children and his ex-wife, Lisbeth. He said he'd call me when he had a chance, but I haven't heard from him yet."

"Well, Mrs. Ramsey was a busy lady today," Marty said. "I told you she'd asked me to go to her home to meet with her this morning. I found out the purpose of my visit was that she wanted to know what I thought the value of Dr. Ramsey's collection was, so she'd have some idea of what to sell it for. I told her since I'd been instructed that the collection belonged to the trust, I couldn't discuss it. She was furious and even offered me a lot of money if I'd tell her, but I turned it down for ethical reasons. In retrospect, that probably wasn't the smartest thing for me to do, considering how much money it cost for my new do."

"Sis, I know you well enough to know that you're only kidding," Laura said. "Jeff, what about Mrs. Ramsey? Does she have an alibi?"

"Yes. I went to her home the night of the murder, and I was the one who told her about his death. She was hosting her monthly bridge club group. There were seven other women there and from what she and the others told me, they'd been playing bridge since three that afternoon. A lot of them play golf most mornings, so the bridge game is at an odd time of day. I don't think there's any way she could have left the game, gone to his office, committed the murder, and returned without anyone noticing her. That really doesn't make sense."

"No, but what if she hired someone to murder him?" Laura asked.

"That's always a definite possibility, but we usually start with the more immediate people of interest. Trying to find a hit person is really difficult. Marty, we all know you had your hair done today and you have a new do, but as I recall, that wasn't the real purpose of your visit to the hair salon, although the results are fabulous, no matter how the rest of your visit went."

"Guys, can you hold that thought?" John said. "I want to hear everything, but Max just gave me the high sign that dinner is ready. We'll be back in a minute with it."

"Actually, that's perfect timing. I see I have an incoming call from Dr. Ramsey's attorney. I'll be back in a couple of minutes as well," Jeff said as he rose from the table and walked towards the gate where he could take the call without the others listening in on what was said.

CHAPTER TWENTY-THREE

"John, I have a deep, dark secret to tell you," Laura said. "I had decided no matter how good the chimichangas were, I was going to tell you that maybe you should make them again, that they weren't quite right. That way I figured I could have them at least one more time," she said with a sigh, "but I just can't do it. That was absolutely the best chimichanga I've ever had. I ate so much, I'll probably never sleep tonight trying to digest it along with the chocolate custard. Once again, you've outdone yourself."

Everyone agreed with Laura's assessment of the chimichangas and the chocolate custard. "Hey everybody, if you get hungry tomorrow, the leftovers will be in my refrigerator. You know I never lock the door to my house, so enjoy."

"Say no more, John. I'll come home for lunch, and I intend to be at the head of the line. You can count on it," Laura said smiling. She turned to Jeff who had returned to the table after taking his phone call. "What did the attorney have to say?"

"It was an interesting conversation. His name is Roger Sills, and he told me Dr. Ramsey and Lisbeth Ramsey were going to reconcile. Dr. Ramsey had met with one of the attorneys in his law office, and his divorce papers had been drawn up, but here's the interesting part. Dr. Ramsey told Roger he was going to tell Ashley he wanted a divorce and that he planned on telling her the night before he was murdered. Quite frankly, I'm not sure what to make of that."

"That goes along with what Lisbeth told me this afternoon," Marty said.

Everyone's head turned in her direction. Jeff was the first to speak. "You never told me you were planning on talking to Lisbeth. Why would you do that?"

"I really hadn't planned on doing it, it just kind of happened. I got to thinking that maybe she knew something. After all, from what we've learned, she seemed to be the love of his life, and I thought maybe she could shed some light on his murder. I didn't have anything in mind, but after I left the hair salon, I drove to her house. When I talked to Sybil after I'd finished lunch and was killing time before my hair appointment, I asked her for Lisbeth's address, which she gave to me. I'm here to tell you she is as beautiful as we've heard, but she is also one of the nicest people I've ever met."

"Did you find out anything?" Jeff asked.

"Not about the murder, but I did find out that for the past six months she and Dr. Ramsey had been seeing each other. She told me she realized she'd made a terrible mistake with the pool guy and that she still loved Dr. Ramsey. They started seeing each other after Lisbeth made up some excuse that she needed to talk to him about their daughter and one thing led to another. He admitted he'd never loved Ashley, and that he'd married her on the rebound. It's really sad to think they were going to reconcile, and then he was murdered."

"So, your opinion of her was favorable?" Laura asked.

"Very. Although I don't have your psychic abilities, I never had any sense that she was other than what she seemed to be, simply a woman who had made a mistake and really regretted it. I don't know what the alimony and child support arrangements were between them, but they must have been pretty good, because she was driving a Ferrari."

"From what Roger told me, she's going to be a very wealthy

woman. According to the trust, she gets half of the doctor's estate, and her children will get the other half. She'll be the guardian of their estate until they reach the age of twenty-one. As such, she'll make all the financial decisions regarding what amount of their trust funds goes for clothes, schooling, and other personal things. He told me he didn't have a final number of what the estate was worth, but he thought it would be in the neighborhood of twenty million dollars. Believe me, that will buy a couple of Ferraris, probably even a fleet."

"Before you all look at me like I'm speaking psychically, I'm not. I am curious, though, whether or not Lisbeth knew she and the children were the beneficiaries of his estate."

"I don't know, Laura," Jeff said. "I had no idea his estate was that large, and although I figured the doctor would provide for his children, I didn't know until I spoke with Roger that his ex-wife would be inheriting half of it." He turned to Marty and said, "You're the one who personally spoke to her. Do you think she knew she'd be named as a beneficiary, and a substantial one at that?"

"No, I never got that sense from her, and I'd be willing to bet she didn't know. I could really be off here, but all I came away with from my meeting with her was a sense of her profound sadness at the tricks life can play on you, such as realizing you made a mistake, admitting it, looking forward to having a second chance at happiness, and then it all blows up and is gone in one devastating moment. Call me a romantic, but I think it's very sad. I believe she really loved him."

They shook their heads in sad agreement, and as if someone had sent out a silent message that it was time to end the evening, they all headed off to their respective houses.

*****

"Jeff, I just thought of something," Marty said as they got ready for bed. "Weren't you going to meet with Dr. Thurston late this afternoon?"

"Yes, and I did," he said as he pulled on his pajamas. As usual, he checked the nightstand next to his side of the bed to make sure his telephone and pistol were on it.

Satisfied, he turned back to her as Marty said, "Want to tell me about it or are you too tired?"

Jeff stretched out on the bed and said, "I really am tired. This feels the best I've felt all day."

Marty laid down next to him and said, "Why don't you tell me while you relax and get ready to go to sleep? I'm curious to find out about all the players." She put her head on his shoulder, and he pulled her to him.

"That's a deal. I'm probably too wound up to go right to sleep anyway, so here's what happened. I went to his office about 4:30 this afternoon. He'd been in surgery since early this morning and was clearly exhausted. He asked if I had a minute, because he'd like to change out of his scrubs. I told him that was fine. He went into the bathroom in his office to change clothes, and while he was in there, I looked around his office."

"I never was in his office when I was doing the appraisal. Anything of interest there?" she asked.

"Depends on what you consider to be of interest," he said as he smoothed back her hair that had fallen onto his face. "The guy is obviously a boat nut. There must have been fifteen photographs of boats, and he was next to a different boat in each one of them. When he came out of the bathroom, I asked him if he'd owned all those boats. They ranged from quite small ones to a couple of pretty large boats."

"Did he?"

"He told me if I looked closely I could see how he'd aged through the years just by looking at the pictures of him next to them. The smaller boats were his first ones, and then he kept moving up to bigger and better ones. I asked him if he was through buying boats, and he told me his dream had always been to own a 40-foot Carver C40. They were built in 2014, and he's wanted one ever since. I looked it up on my iPhone after our meeting, and they are really expensive."

"I've never heard of it, but that's not surprising, considering I don't know anything about boats."

"Nor do I, but I do know that those things cost a lot of money, but what it has to do with Dr. Ramsey's death, that I don't know."

"Okay, Jeff, this is pretty far-fetched, but I haven't heard anything about the business arrangement between Dr. Ramsey and Dr. Thurston. If they were partners, does that mean Dr. Thurston now owns the medical practice?"

"I found out from Sybil that they were not partners. Dr. Thurston essentially rented space and services from Dr. Ramsey. I followed up with Dr. Thurston to hear what he had to say about a business agreement between the two of them. Evidently, they both signed an agreement that in the event one of them could no longer work as a plastic surgeon, then the other one would have the right of first refusal to buy the other's practice."

"Maybe I'm being a little skeptical, Jeff, but wouldn't all, or at least most, of Dr. Ramsey's patients assume that they were partners and just start going to Dr. Thurston?"

He was quiet for several minutes and then said, "Probably, and I think I know where you're going with this. If all of Dr. Ramsey's patients just started going to Dr. Thurston, why would he need to spend the money to buy the practice? Is that what I'm hearing?"

"Well, you said it probably better than I could have put it, but yes, and if that's true, it would sure provide a motive, wouldn't it? If Dr. Thurston kills Dr. Ramsey, he gets Ramsey's patients almost automatically, without having to pay anything. On the other hand, if Ramsey retires or becomes disabled, he has to pay Ramsey to get the practice. Also, if he kills Ramsey, he'll immediately get an increase in income, which will provide the funds he needs to buy the Carver C40 that he wants so badly."

"Yes, it would provide a motive under the scenario you just described, but that's sheer speculation. I got a call today from the lab and there were no fingerprints on the scalpel that was used to kill Dr. Ramsey, other than Dr. Ramsey's. Evidently it was one that he'd used in one of his surgeries."

"Did you ask Dr. Thurston about his diary or little black book?"

"Not specifically. I really couldn't, because he'd probably realize Sybil was the one who'd told me about it. Since Dr. Ramsey almost never entered Dr. Thurston's office, and when he did it was only after checking with Sybil, it wasn't the type of thing Dr. Ramsey would have known about, or probably anyone else, for that matter. I asked him if he used a computer exclusively in his practice or resorted to handwriting notes to himself. He assured me that computers were the best thing that had ever happened to medical practices."

"Where do you go from here?"

"Marty, I wish I had a good answer for that. The chief called me several times today to see what the status of the case was. I guess a lot of the movers and shakers in Palm Springs used the services of Dr. Ramsey, and they're putting pressure on the chief to catch the murderer. You know how political Palm Springs is, and quite frankly, I think the chief is getting a little nervous about his own job."

"I'm so sorry, Jeff. I feel like I failed you today. I really thought I'd find out something that could help you, but I think all I got out of it was a new hairdo."

"Well, my love, at least I know there's one good thing in my life, and that's you. I love you, Marty, and even though your day wasn't as productive as you'd hoped, thanks for trying. Matter of fact, I think I know something that will make me feel even better."

"I may not be psychic like my sister, but even I know what that is, but I have to say, I'm a very willing partner."

It was probably a good thing Jeff had insisted that Duke move to the living room to sleep at night after they got married.

CHAPTER TWENTY-FOUR

The next morning, Marty leaned over and kissed Jeff. "Good morning, sleepy. Thanks for last night, and as a thank you I'll make you breakfast, complete with your favorite food, bacon, right after I walk Duke. How does that sound?"

"Absolutely wonderful. Between us, we've talked to all the persons of interest in the Dr. Ramsey case, and we've drawn a big fat zero. I need to spend the day figuring out how I can solve this case and to do it, I'm definitely going to need some strength which I intend to get from breakfast. Meet you in the kitchen after I shave and shower," he said, grinning at her.

"You're on," Marty said as she pulled her robe around her and headed for the kitchen. A few minutes later, after a short walk with Duke, she was busy stirring waffle batter, frying bacon, cutting up fresh fruit, and cracking eggs for Jeff's breakfast. For the first time in a couple of days she felt like she was doing something worthwhile.

"That was delicious, thank you," Jeff said a little while later. "You certainly know how to start a man's day off on the right note. I honestly think today is the day I'm going to solve this case, at least I hope so."

"Me, too…" she said as Jeff's buzzing phone interrupted her.

He whistled in surprise when he looked at the screen on his phone and saw that the call was from Sybil. He tapped the speaker phone button, so Marty could hear the conversation and said, "Good morning, Sybil, how are you?"

"Detective, I found something you need to know about. Dr. Thurston's the murderer," Sybil said in an hysterical tone of voice.

"Calm down, Sybil, and tell me everything."

"I came in the office as usual this morning. Dr. Thurston and his nursing staff were in surgery, which is also usual at this time of day. He has his early surgery patients use the back door. Anyway, I'd just gotten seated at my desk when his phone rang. His regular staff doesn't come in until a little later, so I answered it. I figured since I'll soon be working for him, it was the least I could do."

"Who was on the phone?"

"It was a yacht broker. He said the owner of the yacht that Dr. Thurston had been looking at had just reduced the price by $20,000, and he wanted the doctor to be the first to know. Evidently Dr. Thurston had told him to call immediately if the price was ever reduced."

"Sybil, you're talking so fast, I'm having trouble understanding you. Please, take a deep breath and try to talk a little slower. I don't want to miss anything."

"Detective, I'm not very proud of what happened next, and as a matter of fact, I'm pretty ashamed of what I did."

"Sybil, please, get on with it."

"All right," she said as she took a deep breath and once again, her words spilled out rapidly. "I knew he'd want to know about the boat's drop in price right away, and since he was in surgery, I took the message from the yacht broker into his office to leave on his desk, so he'd see it first thing when he returned from surgery."

"Well, did you?" Jeff asked.

"Yes and no. I went into his office to leave it, and I saw his diary, which really is a little black book, on his desk. Here's the part I'm not very proud of. I opened it up and read the entries for the last few days. He wrote a detailed description in it of how he murdered Dr. Ramsey," she said as she started to cry.

"Sybil, was there anything in it to indicate why he did it?"

"Yes, he wrote that he and the doctor had argued over Dr. Ramsey attempting to make some of the women he operated on look like Lisbeth. He'd written that while Dr. Ramsey had said he didn't care what they looked like, he, being Dr. Thurston, knew it could eventually affect the practice, and he needed the money from Dr. Ramsey's patients, so he could buy a special boat he wanted. There was a lot more in the diary, but I was afraid he'd come back from surgery and find me in his office reading it, so I took the note from the yacht broker and left his office. Then I called you."

"I'm on my way, Sybil. If you see him when he gets out of surgery, act as normal as you can. If you have a problem, just tell him sometimes you still get affected thinking about Dr. Ramsey's death. I'll be there as soon as I can. I'm going to have several of my men meet me in the parking lot. And Sybil, I can't imagine how hard this must be for you. Thank you. See you as soon as I can get there."

"Oh, Jeff. That poor woman. What can I do?" Marty asked.

"Absolutely nothing," he said as he grabbed his holster and put his pistol in it. A moment later he was out the door. Marty picked up his plate and was walking over to the sink when she heard Laura's voice coming from the direction of the front door.

CHAPTER TWENTY-FIVE

"Marty, open up. I need to talk to you," she heard Laura say from just outside the door.

Marty opened it, and Laura strode into the room. "I just saw Jeff leave. We urgently need to get to Dr. Ramsey's office."

"What are you talking about? Jeff's on his way there now."

"There's no time to waste, Marty. He needs my help," she said as she pushed Marty towards the bedroom. "Quick, get dressed, and we'll leave immediately. I'll tell you all about it on the way there."

Moments later they were headed towards the freeway that led to Palm Desert. "Laura, what's going on? Did you get some message from the other world telling you we need to go there?"

"I had a dream about a little black book last night. It wasn't even like a dream. It was more like I was actually there."

"Laura, I'm missing something. Where were you?"

"At Dr. Ramsey's office. Actually, I was in Dr. Thurston's office. Jeff and some of his detectives were turning the office upside down looking for a black book. I seem to remember that Sybil told you something about Dr. Thurston and a diary. I don't know what the relevance of it is, but I know where it is."

"Keep driving, and I'll tell you about the phone call Jeff just received from Sybil. If you know where it is, it might just be the smoking gun Jeff needs to solve this case and the thing that could lead to Jeff being named as the head of the detectives on the force." She spent the next several minutes telling Laura about the phone conversation she'd heard Jeff having with Sybil.

When they got to the medical building, Laura pulled into the parking lot behind the building and parked. They noticed that the lot had already started to fill up with cars. There were several other doctors who had their offices in the building, and from the looks of the parking lot, a number of patients needed their services. Marty noticed a couple of nondescript cars parked near the back of the lot, and she assumed they belonged to detectives. Jeff's car was there as well.

They opened the door of the medical building and quickly walked down the hall to the reception area of Dr. Ramsey's suite. Several women were seated in the reception room, but Sybil wasn't behind the reception counter. Instead, a young woman Marty recognized from when she'd been there two days earlier was sitting behind the counter. She looked up, smiled, and said, "May I help you?"

"Yes, I know Detective Combs is here. I'm his wife, and I need to speak with him. It's urgent."

"I'm sorry, but Sybil told me they were not to be disturbed," the young woman said.

"Where is Dr. Thurston's office?" Laura asked.

Marty answered, "It's down the hall to the right."

Laura bent down and in a threatening tone of voice, whispered to the young woman, "If you don't open the door, I may not be responsible for what's going to happen in the reception area. Believe me, it will not be a pretty sight, a lot of people are going to get hurt, and I'll make sure to tell everyone that you were the one who caused it." She reached into her purse as if she had a weapon in it.

The terrified young woman whispered, "I'll buzz you in. Please don't do anything. We've had enough to deal with recently."

As Laura and Marty entered the hall behind the reception area, Marty looked down at the young woman and said, "We can find our own way. Believe me, Sybil and the detectives will be very happy we came."

They hurriedly walked down the hall to where they could hear Jeff's firm voice coming from behind a closed door. "Dr. Thurston, you're wasting our time and yours. We know a black book was on your desk earlier this morning. Just tell us where it is, and let's get this over with."

"I don't know what you're talking about." Dr. Thurston said. "To my knowledge, there's never been a black book in this room. Did Sybil tell you there was one? If she did, she's a liar."

It was quiet in the room for a moment, and then they heard Sybil respond. "Dr. Thurston, I saw a black book on your desk this morning when I came into your office to leave a message for you from a yacht broker. It was right in front of your chair."

"My yacht broker called? What did he have to say?" Dr. Thurston asked excitedly.

"Give me the black book, and Sybil will tell you," Jeff said.

"How many times do I have to tell you that there is no black book. I need to go now. My time is very valuable, and you're wasting it. I need to prepare for my next surgery." Marty and Laura heard his voice getting louder, and it sounded like he was walking towards the door they were standing behind.

Laura swung the door open and said, "Jeff, I know where the black book is. I don't know what's in it, but I think you better restrain the doctor while I find it."

Jeff nodded to the two men who were standing next to Dr.

Thurston. Each of them took one of the doctor's arms while Laura strode across the room to a bookcase located on the back wall of the office. She stood on her tiptoes and retrieved a book from the upper shelf. She opened it, flipped through several pages, and then carefully removed a black book from a plastic sleeve that had been glued to one of the pages in the book. She turned and handed the small black book to Jeff.

"I think this is the black book you're looking for," Laura said.

Jeff looked at Sybil as he took the book from Laura and said, "Sybil, is this the one you saw earlier?"

She walked over to Jeff, looked at it, and said, "Yes, Detective, that's it."

"This is ridiculous," Dr. Thurston said. "Someone must have planted a black book in one of my medical research books. I don't know anything about this."

Jeff leafed through the last few pages of the book and caught his breath. The room was quiet while he read several of them, then he looked up and said, "Tell you what, Doctor, I want to hear you say that again after we have our handwriting analyst examine this little book and compare it to your handwriting. When that's been completed, based on what I just read, you're going to be charged with the murder of Dr. Keith Ramsey. Right now, I'm placing you under arrest, and my men are going to take you to the station for questioning."

As Jeff's detectives escorted Dr. Thurston out of his office, he looked at Sybil and said, "You're fired. I wouldn't ever have anyone like you work for me. I'll soon be getting a much better administrative assistant, one that's loyal and that I can trust."

When they'd left, Jeff said, "Sybil, I think you're going to have to look for another job. Dr. Thurston isn't going to be practicing medicine again. Those days are over for him, and so are his days on his boat. I know you have plenty to do with cancelling more appointments, but I want you to know how much I appreciate what you did. You could have decided to ignore the book and keep your job. No one would have known. Because of you, justice will be served."

"Detective, I don't know what to think about any of this. It's been the worst few days of my life. After I see to some of the more immediate fires that need to be put out, I want to take a little time off and figure out what I'm going to do with the rest of my life." She walked out the door and back to the surgery center, presumably to tell the woman who was expecting to be operated on shortly, that her surgery was being delayed, and it might be a long delay.

Jeff turned to where Marty and Laura were standing. "Laura, I can only assume that you were given some information psychically, but I don't know how I'm going to explain it to the chief, or anyone else, for that matter."

"I had a dream last night, Jeff. Actually, it was more than a dream. I was in this office, and I saw Dr. Thurston put the black book in the sleeve in the book on the top shelf. How it happened, I have no idea, but then I never do."

"This is way beyond me, but all I know is that you really saved my case. I was going nowhere with this, and I'm not sure Dr. Thurston would have been at the top of my list of suspects. I need to get in touch with the psychiatrist the police force works with as well as our handwriting expert. Dr. Thurston didn't appear to have any major psychological problems, so it looks like he'll be able to stand trial for Dr. Ramsey's murder."

"I don't know, Jeff. Seems to me you have to be insane to murder someone for a boat. That's hardly a crime of passion," Marty said.

"Yeah, that's always a tough call. I need to get to the station, and I know I have a long day ahead of me. See you tonight. You can tell the others what happened. It will save me the trouble. I have enough to do at the moment, and Laura, once again, I owe you my everlasting thanks."

"Tell you what, Jeff, a client of ours swears by Patron tequila. If you can get John to make chimichangas again, and we drink the Patron with it, I'll consider it a fair exchange."

"For you, dear sister-in-law, anything. Consider it done!"

EPILOGUE

Several days later, Jeff knocked on Laura's door before he left for work. "Laura, don't be late for dinner tonight. I've talked to John, and he's making chimichangas for you. I'm holding up my part of the bargain, since I bought the best Patron tequila I can afford. See you at dinner."

That evening the five residents of the compound and Max met at the outdoor table in the courtyard under the tree with the sparkling lights.

"Okay, everyone, here's the Patron tequila Laura asked for. I did a little research, and it should be sipped. In Mexico, where it comes from, the people like to drink it in sips they call 'little kisses' or '*besitos*,' but first a toast to Laura." Jeff turned towards her and said, "To the best sister-in-law in the world and the reason I was officially named today as the head of the detective division for the Palm Springs Police Department." He looked around at all of them, a big grin on his face.

Marty was sitting next to him, looking at him with a wide-eyed expression, and then she said excitedly, "Jeff, that's fabulous. You never said a word to me. Is it effective immediately?" she asked as she kissed him on the cheek and squeezed his hand.

"Effective as of today, and so is the pay raise. Well, what do you all think? Is Laura's choice to go with the chimichangas a good one?"

"Excellent," Les said. "What's the latest on the Dr. Ramsey murder case?"

"Quite a bit, actually. Our psychiatrist found that Dr. Thurston has hypergraphia, which is a behavioral condition often associated with epilepsy. He simply can't help himself from writing down in great detail pretty much everything that happens to him every day. It was lucky for us, because his condition caused him to write down that he murdered Dr. Ramsey, and why. Our handwriting analysis expert determined that the handwriting in the black book is his." Jeff stopped talking long enough to take a sip of his Patron.

"Now what happens?" Laura asked.

"He'll stand trial for Dr. Ramsey's murder. The District Attorney doesn't think he'll be able to get off with a plea of insanity, but I'm sure his attorney will try. We'll see."

"How's Sybil doing? Have you talked to her recently?" Marty asked.

"Yes, as a matter of fact I touched base with her a little while ago. She's still hurting, but when all the other plastic surgeons in the area found out she was available, she had her choice of twelve different job offers. She accepted one and seems quite happy with it."

"What about Dr. Ramsey's wives?" Laura asked.

"Wife number two, Lisbeth, is devoted to her children and wants to keep the memory of their father intact for them. I think she'll make a very good financial guardian of their estates until they reach age twenty-one. Since I didn't want her or her children to hear the news on television, I went to her home the day we discovered that Dr. Thurston was the murderer. I have to agree with everyone's assessment, she really is a beauty."

"I wonder if she'll find someone else," Marty said.

"Well, sweetheart, you did, and you'd sworn off men. I'd say if you could succumb to a man's charms, Lisbeth will too."

"Jeff, I'm going to pretend I didn't hear that. It sounds a little too male chauvinistic for me."

"Okay, I apologize. It was probably a combination of a really good day and the Patron."

"Back to the wives," Laura said. "What about Ashley? What's going to happen to her?"

"Don't know. When I talked to Roger Sills recently, he said she'd moved out of the house, since the trust specified that it go to his children and Lisbeth. He said the three of them are going to move into the house, because Lisbeth wants the children to be familiar with their father's heritage, and she could think of no better way than through his antique Shaker collection. She's arranging for the pieces in his office to be integrated with the others in their home."

"That pretty well sums up the whole group, doesn't it?" Marty asked.

"I think we've accounted for everyone, even Duke here," he said petting the dog who was resting his big head on Jeff's thigh. "I'd swear I just heard a knock at the gate. Marty, would you mind getting that while I pour a little more Patron for everyone, although I can't imagine who it could be at this time of night." As Marty walked over to the gate, Jeff winked at Laura.

A moment later Marty walked back into the courtyard with tears in her eyes and a little bundle of white fur in her arms. "Jeff, she's about the most adorable puppy I've ever seen," she said as she looked down at the little white boxer in her arms.

"First of all, she is a he," he said grinning, "and secondly your psychic sister picked up that you were a little jealous of my new relationship with Duke and felt you needed a little something for yourself. Being the wonderful husband that I am, I felt that was the least I could do for someone who helped me solve the Ramsey murder case. I know you'll enjoy the new addition to our family."

Marty looked up at him and said, "This is the best surprise in the world. What shall we name him?"

Les looked over at the bottle of Patron and said, "Patron, what else? Then he'll always be celebrated."

"Good choice, my friend," Jeff said holding up his glass. "One more toast, my friends, to Patron!"

RECIPES

MEXICAN CHOCOLATE CUSTARD

Ingredients:
2/3 cup sugar
1/4 cup cornstarch
1/3 cup Dutch-processed unsweetened cocoa powder
Two tbsp. Mexican chocolate (I like the Iberra brand.)
3 cups whole milk
6 large egg yolks (I like to use the jumbo eggs, rather than large.)
2 ¼ tsp. vanilla extract (Please don't use the imitation. It really makes a difference)
Whipped cream (Optional)

Directions:
In a 2-quart saucepan, whisk the sugar, cornstarch, cocoa, Mexican chocolate, milk, and egg yoks together until the mixture is smooth. Place the pan over medium heat and stir in the vanilla. Bring to a low boil and simmer for 5 minutes. Transfer the mixture to a glass bowl and place plastic wrap on the top to keep a skin from forming. Refrigerate until chilled, about 3 hours. When ready to serve top with a dollop of whipped cream. Enjoy!

MAMA'S MEATBALLS

Ingredients:
1 cup fresh bread crumbs (I just tear fresh bread up into small pieces.)
½ cup milk
1 lb. ground beef
1 lb. ground pork
1 ½ tsp. sea salt
½ tsp. freshly ground pepper
2/3 cup finely chopped onion
2 large eggs (I like to use jumbo.)
½ cup (1 stick) unsalted butter (Always use unsalted. Otherwise whatever you're making can become way too salty.)
Vegetable oil for frying
2 tbsp. all-purpose flour
2 cups beef broth (You can use canned, homemade, or made from cubes.)
½ cup heavy cream

Directions:
Place the bread crumbs in a small bowl and soak in the milk for 15 minutes. Squeeze the moisture out. In a large bowl mix the bread, beef, pork, onion, eggs, salt, and pepper until blended. Form this mixture into small balls about 1 ½" round, and place them on a cookie sheet. (If you like to make things ahead of time, you can make them to this point and hold them in the refrigerator for 2 days.)

Preheat the oven to 250 degrees. In a large frying pan, melt half of the butter and add enough vegetable oil to it, so that it's about ½" deep in the pan. When the foam from the butter subsides, cook several meatballs at a time for about 10 minutes, browning on all sides. Repeat until all of the meatballs have been cooked. When each batch is completed, transfer them to a paper towel lined cookie sheet. Place them in the oven to keep warm while finishing the recipe.

Pour the fat out of the pan and add the remaining butter to it. Whisk the flour in until bubbles form on the surface. Continue to cook, whisking constantly, for 3 more minutes. Slowly add in the broth and bring to a boil. Pour the cream into the sauce and bring to a gentle simmer. Add the meatballs and simmer until warm. Transfer mixture to a large serving bowl and enjoy!

NOTE: These are particularly good served over rice or noodles. If you'd like to make the meatballs larger, adjust the frying time upwards until cooked through.

CHIMICHANGAS

Ingredients:
1 lb. ground beef
1 16 oz. can refried beans
½ cup finely chopped onion
24 oz. tomato sauce
2 tsp. chili powder (If you don't like things spicy, start with 1 tsp. When the mixture is cooking, taste it and adjust to your taste buds.)
1 tsp. minced garlic
½ tsp. ground cumin
12 10" flour tortillas
1 4 oz. can chopped chilies
1 4 oz. can chopped jalapeno peppers (As above, if you don't like things too spicy, start with half of the chilies and peppers. Taste while the mixture is cooking and add more if desired.)
Vegetable oil for deep fat frying
1 ½ cups shredded sharp cheddar cheese
Tin foil

Directions:
Preheat oven to 250 degrees. Wrap the tortillas in tin foil and warm in the oven until ready to use. (Don't skip this step. If the tortillas are not warm, they are much harder to fold when you get ready to fill them – that's from personal experience!)

In a large skillet cook the ground beef until it's no longer pink. Drain the fat from the pan and stir in the beans, onions, ½ cup tomato sauce, chili powder, garlic, and cumin.

Spoon about 1/3 cup of the mixture onto a tortilla slightly to one side of center. Fold the edge of the tortilla up and over the mixture to cover. Fold in bottom sides and roll up. Secure with toothpicks.

Sauce:
In a saucepan over medium heat mix the remaining tomato sauce with the chilies and peppers. Keep warm until ready to serve.

In a large deep fry pan heat 1" oil to 375 degrees. Fry the chimichangas for about 2 minutes on each side or until brown. (I've made the mistake of not having the oil hot enough and they didn't get as brown and crisp as they should.)

Drain on paper towels. (I usually do them in batches and then put them in the oven to keep warm while I finish the others.) Spoon a small amount of the sauce on the top of each one. Finish with a sprinkle of cheese. Serve with the remaining sauce at the table. Enjoy!

RED RICE

Ingredients:
2 tbsp. olive oil
2 cups finely chopped brown onions
1 cup seeded and finely chopped red bell pepper
1 6 oz. can tomato sauce
3 cups chicken broth (You can use canned, homemade, or cubes)
1 tbsp. sugar
½ tsp. freshly ground black pepper
1 1/2 cups converted long grain rice

Directions:
In a 4-quart saucepan, heat the oil over medium heat. Add the onions and bell pepper. Cook until soft, about 3 minutes. Add the tomato sauce, chicken broth, sugar, and black pepper. Stir to blend. Bring to a boil, reduce the heat to medium, and simmer for 10

minutes. Add the rice, cover, and reduce the heat to low. Simmer until the liquid is completely absorbed, about 30 minutes. Serve and enjoy!

BUTTERMILK FRIED CHICKEN

Ingredients:
10 pieces of chicken, thighs and drumsticks
4 cups buttermilk
3 tbsp. kosher salt
2 tsp. freshly ground pepper
1 ½ cups all-purpose flour
3 cups oil (I like to use peanut oil, but canola or vegetable oil is fine.)

Directions:
Place chicken in large dish and cover with buttermilk. Sprinkle with 2 tbsp. salt and a couple of grinds of fresh pepper. Cover with plastic wrap and refrigerate for at least one hour or up to one day. (I like to marinate it for a day. I think it's better to do it a little longer.) Remove from the refrigerator and bring to room temperature.

Combine flour, remaining salt, and pepper in a large dish or a paper bag. (I've found a paper bag is the easiest way to coat the chicken.) Shake the bag or turn the chicken pieces in the flour to uniformly coat them.

Pour the oil into a heavy-bottomed deep pan with high sides and a lid, to a depth of 3". Heat the oil over medium-high heat to 350 degrees.

Preheat the oven to 250 degrees if you plan on serving the chicken warm. Set a baking rack on a baking sheet. Shake the excess flour off the chicken pieces and fry them in batches, skin side down, with the lid on. You don't want to crowd them. Cook for 10 to 15 minutes, until browned. Remove the lid, turn the pieces, and cook for an additional 10 to 15 minutes. (Remember, ranges vary. If the chicken is cooking faster or slower, the color is more important than the time. You're looking for a golden brown.)

When cooked, place the cooked pieces on the rack, drain, and keep warm in the oven. (If you're going to serve it cold or at room temperature, you can eliminate this step.) Serve and enjoy!

Paperbacks & Ebooks for FREE

Go to www.dianneharman.com/freepaperback.html and get your FREE copies of Dianne's books and favorite recipes immediately by signing up for her newsletter.

Once you've signed up for her newsletter you're eligible to win three paperbacks. One lucky winner is picked every week. Hurry before the offer ends!

ABOUT THE AUTHOR

Dianne lives in Huntington Beach, California, with her husband, Tom, a former California State Senator, and her boxer dog, Kelly. Her passions are cooking, reading, and dogs, so whenever she has a little free time, you can either find her in the kitchen, playing with Kelly in the back yard, or curled up with the latest book she's reading.

Her award winning books include:

Cedar Bay Cozy Mystery Series
Kelly's Koffee Shop, Murder at Jade Cove, White Cloud Retreat, Marriage and Murder, Murder in the Pearl District, Murder in Calico Gold, Murder at the Cooking School, Murder in Cuba, Trouble at the Kennel, Murder on the East Coast, Trouble at the Animal Shelter, Murder & The Movie Star

Liz Lucas Cozy Mystery Series
Murder in Cottage #6, Murder & Brandy Boy, The Death Card, Murder at The Bed & Breakfast, The Blue Butterfly, Murder at the Big T Lodge, Murder in Calistoga

High Desert Cozy Mystery Series
Murder & The Monkey Band, Murder & The Secret Cave, Murdered by Country Music, Murder at the Polo Club, Murdered by Plastic Surgery

Midwest Cozy Mystery Series
Murdered by Words, Murder at the Clinic

Jack Trout Cozy Mystery Series
Murdered in Argentina

Northwest Cozy Mystery Series
Murder on Bainbridge Island, Murder in Whistler

Coyote Series
Blue Coyote Motel, Coyote in Provence, Cornered Coyote

Midlife Journey Series
Alexis

Website: www.dianneharman.com, **Blog:** www.dianneharman.com/blog
Email: dianne@dianneharman.com

Newsletter

If you would like to be notified of her latest releases please go to www.dianneharman.com and sign up for her newsletter.